ECHOES OF EUNOIA

By: Daze Evander

PREFACE

Years ago I had a dream that inspired me to write this story.

Exploration of the mind can be similar to navigating a mysterious planet.

Every person has a unique point of view in trying to pursue their dreams and wishes.

Our thoughts can shape our perspectives in a way that completely alters the world around us.

Thank you so much for taking the time to read my book.

I hope you enjoy the second half of Eunoia.

Daze Evander

CONTENTS

LIST OF ACKNOWLEDGEMENTS:

Special thanks to all of the artists:

Front and Back Cover: **James Child**

Character Portraits: **Kevin Sardinha**

Planet Map: **Kkalmighty**

PLANET MAP

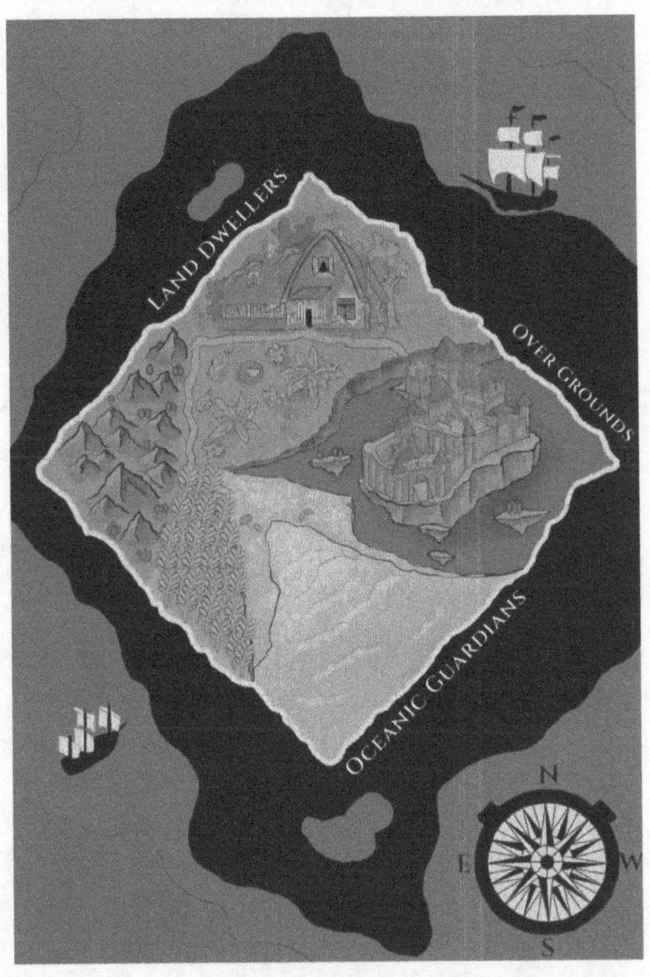

CHAPTER ONE: COLD AWAKENING

Zayika

Six Weeks Before

"You will regret this Anon. I will never forget you." Zayika spoke hauntingly. "I promise that I will find a way to make you regret this."

The Over Grounds representative used a supernatural ability to transport Amira and Anon back to Earth with one quick hand movement. A bright light engulfed everyone… and then the two were gone. Zayika laid on the ground, trying to comprehend the devastation of unprecedented betrayal. Both women made eye contact for a tense minute, unsure of what words to use to break the festering silence. A storm was forming on planet Eunoia. Chilling wind blew around in circles against their long hair and shivering bodies. The sky transitioned into a dark tone of purple, decorated with what looked to be the shapes of several white eyes within the asperitas clouds above them.

"What's going on?" Zayika asked.

"I'm not sure." the representative responded.

There were sounds of crackling lightning and bellowing thunder beginning as Zayika stood up to regain her composure. "Take me to Earth too. I'm right here and ready to go!"

Her faction leader was distraught. "I can't do that."

"What do you mean? Don't tell me that you're as awful as Amira and Anon. I know that you can help me, you're just refusing to."

"It's not that."

"Then what is it?" Zayika's voice was shrill.

"You would never understand." she said fearfully and looked at the two other leaders from the Oceanic Guardian and Land Dweller groups. "We have to go." Her hand was raised once again.

"Where?" Zayika stomped forwards. "Take me with yo—"

The three disappeared before her plea was finished as smoke could be seen where each of them had stood, leaving her alone on the cold ocean shore. Many days started to pass by and she was left having to face her thoughts and decide what path to take next. She took the leftover food and water from the abandoned Land Dweller faction and paraded around in her thoughts. After spending a great deal of time walking around, she discovered that she had a useful capability that allowed her to conjure stars from anywhere within her body and used them to get past a variety of obstacles in her way. Zayika tried out everything that she learned. Boiling stars could be launched from all her fingertips, soft ones were able to heal wounds, and she even discovered how to create a cloud from below her feet to glide on for accessing hard to reach places. It seemed to her that the possibilities were endless and that there was still a lot more to uncover.

Eventually the planet's coldness started to bother her. Zayika grew tired of the effort it took to consistently keep warm with her ability, so she decided to go to the Over Ground faction and see if there were any clothes left to find. She reached the front doors by riding up into the sky since the wall was damaged and unclimbable. It took a few attempts, but eventually she was able to keep her balance and use the puff of stars underneath her feet to skate past the challenging surfaces. The floating castle was vacant and broken. She went through each room and made sure to check for anything that could be of use and tore off what chips were left of white nail polish on her fingers. After a few minutes of browsing wardrobes, she stumbled upon a white and grey long sleeve turtleneck dress. It fit her perfectly as she fastened it alongside her trembling skin and immediately started to feel its warmth.

A mirror in the room showed a reflection of herself standing strikingly in the new outfit. Zayika's dress fell slightly over the black boots that reached the top of her thighs. She whispered one simple sentence of vengeance while staring ahead, "Revenge isn't complete without consequences."

Present

Planet Eunoia became my home. I would keep track of how many days were passing as a burning feeling arose within me after being left behind on it. Every minute felt like an hour. I didn't know how long it had been since the wishes were used. The colors of the sky changed from a greenish blue to the same purple hue I dyed my hair.

There were relentless bouts of wind that would follow me around as I ventured in circles and tried to organize my thoughts. The three representatives of the factions who also abandoned me were still somewhere on the planet. I was completely alone, unsure of where they were, and also feeling as though I was searching for a piece of my own self. *Is anyone else going to be brought here from Earth like I was? Will they be able to after Amira destroyed that waterfall?*

The realization that everything would be stripped of me, especially my potential, became overwhelming. Seeking the revenge that coursed through my veins was inevitable. Eunoia did not feel empty… its jungle, ocean, castles… everything was full of opportunity.

Intrusive thoughts wouldn't go away. I could see Amira and Anon's faces laughing at me. *I should've obliterated them when I had the chance.* Hatred began to brew. *I should have fought Anon when he tried to defend Amira.* I used to care about going back to Earth like they did, but that changed. I was wronged and needed to clear my name. *Make everything right.* There was a set of words completely stuck in my mind on a loop. *How could he, how could he, how could he?* I was in a manic state for a very long time. Anon was the worst person I ever met and Amira was runner up. The two of them left me stranded to die on a planet festering with loneliness, tortured souls, and lost hope. Neither deserved to remain alive, let alone have the wishes they used to screw me over. *Make him pay, make him pay, make him —* the words changed.

I laughed out loud in the darkness and heard the planet join in. The sounds of our mutual joy echoed. I ran mindlessly in the night over moist vines, past the unexplored ocean, and near the damaged floating castle. I was left with so much time on my hands and therefore used my fingers to keep track of dark fantasies. I allowed myself to imagine ten times per day how I would kill Anon. *Space them out.* He was a reckless human that ruined my chance to finish solving problems back on Earth. *None of that matters anymore.* Thankfully my priorities had changed. My issue was not with other people I used to know in the past, but with him. He was the last person I saw when a gust of light left a searing ache behind my eyes that wouldn't go away. Actions had consequences and there were too many people on Eunoia who weren't served them. A wicked smile met my lips. *Someone has to serve justice, right?*

I was hopeful that I could bring him back. *There has to be a way to manipulate time and space.* Then the brilliant idea hit me. *The representatives.* One of them acquired the power to transport someone from the planet I was on back to Earth. The Over Grounds representative took Anon and Amira home. *I have to keep her alive.* The other two, from the Land Dweller and Oceanic Guardian factions, were expendable to me. They contributed nothing of any substance. I decided to hunt them down and test out my abilities I hadn't gotten to fully try out yet.

I could heal with stars and used them to fix one of Anon's life-threatening wounds. *Definitely regret doing that now. There are cases in which my acts of kindness don't matter. Some who receive them won't feel inclined to owe me anything back.* My mindset shifted towards a desire to discover how much I could make someone else suffer. *I can heal myself, which will come in handy.* My first target was the Land Dweller's representative, who I assumed would be easier to find than the one in the ocean. *What is it that they do while we all attack one another? Sit and watch? Take bets on who will survive? I pity any who put money on Omar… or even Saige.*

I wove through the freezing jungle by tip-toeing quietly in my boots. The dress I found in my faction's headquarters did an amazing job at keeping me warm, like my adrenaline. The representatives knew I was left on the planet with them, but were unsure of what I would do… and scared to find out. They were trying to stay under the radar until another batch of hopeful and unprepared contenders arrived from Earth. Then they'd force them into groups, morph them, and watch everyone fight. *What happens when the roles are reversed?*

I finally stumbled across my first victim. The Land Dweller was parting ways with the representative from my faction. The two were finishing a conversation which seemed to be concerned with important matters since they acted as if they were strategizing something. I stood in the shadows of thick vines as I waited for the woman to leave. The anticipation of what was to come was thrilling.

"Hey." I said excitedly when she was finally gone.

His eyes searched for where I was speaking from. "Zayika, is that you?"

I stepped towards him gracefully as I replied, "Who else would it be?"

"I'm not sure. Anything is possible."

"Let's cut the small talk. I think we should play a game." I was clicking my fingernails against one another, highly anticipating the act of releasing pent up frustration on someone else.

"No thanks. You should be waiting for others to arrive."

"I don't really care about that. They won't be able to give me what I want, what I need, so I won't waste my time on them."

"I wouldn't be so positive about those words." he rocked back and forth on his heels. "The... failed experiments have been given to our crocodile, but those who survived became magical beings after surviving the morphing process just like you. You have no idea who may be brought here next—or what abilities they may gain."

"Wait. What 'crocodile' are you talking about?" I asked him.

"Of course you wouldn't know. At one edge of the planet, in the pond beside my faction, is an uncontrollable mutant who spawned along with Hippo as the planet came into existence. It took us some time to discover his purpose, but once we did it changed everything. Hippo was designed to take care of unwelcome oceanic creatures and this reptile was made to dispose of the potential fighters we've lost. Both can also fight alongside a faction member—as you may have seen with the anglerfish. But on my terrain so far, well, those who died while being morphed simply got tossed into the crocodile's mouth to be chewed up and digested. It gets more powerful with each feeding."

"Seriously? Wow. Seems like a great way to get rid of somebody." I smiled at the thought of chucking Anon into it like an activated wood chipper. "Though I don't understand something. How could anyone else get here? Amira destroyed the waterfall... you don't remember that?"

He snickered. "I remember, but it turns out she did nothing at all with her wish, not like we were fearing."

"You all were shaking with dread at what she chose."

"Yes. I vividly recall wincing at that wish being granted and fearful that my life was going to end. Destroying the waterfall could have resulted in the entire planet being tarnished. That location was the portal which created the gateway to this place after all."

What he was saying would have probably been very interesting to someone else, though it wasn't to me. I was only concerned with one thing: using my ability for revenge. I needed to get Anon and possibly Amira back if I could, but wanted to practice my powers before trying to call them back to Eunoia.

I clicked my tongue against the roof of my mouth and walked closer to the representative. "What is your life really worth anyways?"

"Excuse me?" He put a hand up to his chest with an offended look.

"You just sit around on this planet and eat scraps from your treehouse days on end for what reason? What are you truly gaining? Were you brought here against your will and you've lost your mind in the process, too? Are you being blackmailed?"

"This place is my calling."

"The three of you representatives don't make sense to me." I tossed all of my hair over one shoulder.

"You might not understand what it means to have a greater purpose like we do, to belong somewhere which seems impossible, but that's because of your own limitations. The three of us stand by what we've built and have a duty to contribute to the vision of this planet."

I rolled my eyes. "I've wasted enough time talking about all of this with you. Can you help me use my ability?"

"We're from different factions. I don't feel like helping you." He scoffed and crossed his arms.

I felt my lips curl into a smile as I responded, "Great answer. Thanks for reminding me that I have nothing to lose by eliminating you."

"'Eliminating' me? You're quite confident, aren't you?"

"There is nothing wrong with having confidence." I told him.

"You won't hurt me."

"Don't be so sure about that."

I brought stars from my hands that formed a floating orb at my fingertips. They fizzled and shone brightly with vibrancy that bounced off my face.

"What are you going to do with that?" He laughed. "You're a healer, aren't you? Like you could even—"

I hurled the orb directly at his body with full force, leaning into a deep lunge as I did so. "Is this a joke to you?"

The stars I cast scattered across his skin and tore it away layer by layer. He yelled out in anguish as my ability ripped him to shreds. I was tempted to heal him and try again to see what other things I could do, but decided to be patient for the others I would fight.

"Help me! Please! Everything stings!" he said while being completely skinned alive and staring at me with desperate eyes.

I should put him out of his misery. There's no use in torturing him. I closed my eyes and formed another orb of stars with the intent for them to explode. As they hit him again he erupted from the inside out. I was launched away from the shockwave and fell onto my back. His body parts were scattered all around. Breathing heavily, I felt a surge of adrenaline kick me into full force. *I am capable of anything.* I knew where to go next.

There was an obstacle to deal with when I went to find the Oceanic Guardian representative. *She is submerged right now... isn't she?* I didn't have the ability to breathe underwater since I did not belong to that faction, but I was sure that my stars could still help me find out where she was down in the ocean. *I don't need to get in there. Create a spotlight and force her out.* I rolled my shoulders back and forth as I reactivated my ability. With palms directed outwards, I began to force out a multitude of stars, not taking a break for even a second, and they started to fill the waves. The entire ocean was slowly being lit up.

No way... I spotted the Oceanic Guardians' castle, sea life that I didn't know existed, and several statues with moss growing all over them. There were also a few swimming creatures nearby that made themselves at home. *This is beautiful.* The ocean went from dark blue to bright white and yellow at the cause of my own hands. I stared ahead to take in the sight. Thankfully the light nudged her out of hiding as she retreated from her comfort zone by exiting the castle and up to the surface.

"Hey!" I called out after her. "We need to talk to each other!"

"Me?" she responded.

"Yes." *There's only a few of us on this planet... who do you think I'm talking to?*

"What is going on? I can hardly see anything!" With hesitation, she used her long tail to swim her way to the shore. I tried to keep my morbid anticipation hidden. She came out of the water and didn't take her eyes off of mine. While she laid on the sand waiting for her scales to fall off, I put my hand down to shake hers.

"I'm not sure we've properly met each other. I'm Zayika. You probably recognize me."

"Yes I do. How could I forget your face?" Her eyes looked upset. "It was a bit surprising that you were left behind, but don't worry, we will eventually have another opening ceremony with new participants."

"I don't really care about that anymore."

"Well you should. You'll have a whole new chance to go home."

"My home is here now." I was surprised at how naturally those words flew out of my mouth. "There is business I need to focus on."

"Like what? What could you possibly need to do besides wait for the next batch of fighters to arrive?"

"I need to practice using the abilities I was given when morphed. The Land Dweller representative assisted me a little bit, but I also want some guidance from you."

"Oh… Aadavan. Yes, he's very helpful, I'm glad to hear that." She finally shook my hand. "My name is Lorelai. Is there anything you want specific training with?"

"Yes." I started to fire off rounds of stars at her face. "I need to know how to defeat someone very efficiently."

She dodged the first two shots. "What are you doing? Why are you attacking me? Have you lost your mind?"

"I think so, but I gave up on looking for it a long time ago."

Four Months Before

"Zayika, what are you doing?" her friend Andrea sprang out of the passenger's seat.

"Don't interfere with my plan. You don't want to get in the way." Zayika gave her a threatening look as they stood near the curb.

"I can't sit by and watch you do something… that you'll regret. Nothing about this seems right."

Rain was pouring heavily over the two women, their hair and clothes drenched as both of them stared at each other with vastly different expressions. Storm clouds filled the sky and traveled fast as though they were racing one another.

Zayika put her fingers up to her mouth and tapped them against her lips. "This isn't what it looks like."

"You have a weapon in your hand that I can see quite clearly. Please take me home."

"What will you do if I don't?"

"I'll call the cops." Andrea pulled her phone out of her pocket. "Literally."

Zayika looked upwards and noticed how the street lights closest to them were dimly flickering, their bulbs almost about to die. "I won't let you do that. Just come with me, okay? I'll explain everything once we talk to the others. There's no need to involve law enforcement when consequences can be dealt out and handled between the two parties involved."

"Why are you acting like this? We were supposed to enjoy my birthday tonight, not hunt down everyone else who made other plans."

"I'll give you one more chance. Do you want to join me or not?" Zayika was growing impatient.

"Okay. Fine. I'll go with you to see what you want to show me… but if I want to leave then I will."

"You'll be happy that you came along. Trust me. I don't make choices without thinking about them first. There is order to my actions."

Present

Lorelai realized quite suddenly that she needed to protect herself. *At least she isn't going to waste time with needless talking.* I was ready to fight.

"Zayika." She started to bring waves up high into the sky from behind her at the twitching of her fingertips. "Please think before you act on your emotions. I understand that you are lonely and feel misinterpreted by everyone who meets you."

"You're wrong. How could you possibly assume to know that about me?"

"Because something similar happened to me years ago when I fought on this planet."

She's lying. She was not a fighter. Lorelai is trying to play a pathos card. All she wants to do is appeal to my emotions. I wasn't buying the approach she was taking.

"Let's get this over with for the sake of saving time." I took note of her ability. "So you can control water? Interesting. I would have never guessed." I said sarcastically.

"I can command sea creatures too. Don't make me use more of my powers against you."

As she threw her arms forward to send what looked to be sharpened waves towards me, I tested out my stars against them. I was able to stop her attack with closed fists. I clenched so hard that my own nails tore and dug through my palms. My stars began to evaporate the water and became even brighter than before. She couldn't help but look at the intense light behind her.

"What are you doing? How are you..." She was mesmerized.

"I'm the product of a morphing process gone extremely well."

Lorelai's attention was glued to the brightness. The waves jostled alongside what I was doing and it got to the point where she was completely overtaken with them. I didn't realize how truly powerful I was but began to understand the scope of what I could do. She fell to her knees in the ocean, which made her tail start to reappear. While her focus was stuck on the vibrant waves, I walked up behind her and used my scalding hot fingers and long nails to gouge her eyes out. I finished her off with another exploding orb while she cried out for help.

Only one representative left. After throwing her body into the ocean, I used the water to clean off the blood splatter on my hands and outfit to regain my composure. As my breathing slowed, I saw a figure move swiftly in my peripheral vision—thankfully I noticed the direction she was heading in. *That's the last one. She was watching me.*

My hunt came to an end when I found the last representative in an oceanside cave. It was easy to reach her clever hideout thanks to the use of directing stars to flow through my feet. A layer of them formed underneath me and I traveled on top of them to breeze past wet rocks to the edge of the cliff. I felt another surge of excitement. *Did she really think I wouldn't come after her, too?* Once I reached the top, I looked behind me at the roaring waves and grey clouds looming in the sky. I ran my fingers through my hair while I stepped closer to her.

"Knock, knock." I leaned against rocks at the cave's opening. "I know that someone is home."

"What? How did you find me?" she said, crawling out from the shaded area.

"You made it obvious where you were going." I answered. "So how should we do this?"

Let's see if she wants to make this challenging.

"Why are you hunting us? I saw you kill Lorelei and Aadavan! You really should not have done that! Zayika you don't know how valuable they were. Those two were the best representatives this planet will ever have."

"What makes you think I care?" I asked with a blank stare. "Besides, they couldn't even defend themselves. Who's to say Hippo wouldn't have killed them on a bad day when she gets bored or sick of eating other fish?"

"You're trying to bend the rules here... and you shouldn't."

"Why is that?"

"I remember the look in your eyes when you were left behind at the closing ceremony, in fact, I will never forget it. Amira and Anon decided to team up and left you abandoned and shattered on the ground."

"Do you think I don't know this?" It was making me upset to relive the moment by her words.

"Of course I know that you do. You're not as guarded as you seem to think, Zayika, you're actually quite transparent."

I stood taller. "What is that supposed to mean?"

"I can see how damaged you are over Anon. You saved that man's life two times and sacrificed your own safety to help. You were selfless which made you vulnerable."

I rolled my eyes so hard that it hurt. "Anon means nothing to me. Stop reading into nonsense."

"If what you just said was the truth... then why do you care so much about what he chose to do with his wish?"

"You don't even know what you are talking about!" I clapped my hands together. "He left me behind—that's why I care. Yes, I saved his useless life. I swam into that disgusting and dangerous ocean after he made yet another bad decision, but I only did so because I knew I could hold it over his head and have a favor done for me in return. I want people to owe me something which is the only reason why I've ever helped anybody! It's one of the ways I look out for myself."

She glanced down at her feet. "We could talk in circles and get nowhere. I won't waste anymore words on you even though I think you need to hear them. What is it that you want with me?"

"I want you to bring Anon back here to Eunoia."

"Why? What will that accomplish?"

"I don't have to explain myself to you, you're not my therapist." I quickly spouted out in her direction. I had to be quick on my feet and tongue if I wanted to survive and get what I needed. *Some things never change.*

"I can't just bring him back here." she told me. "There are rules to Eunoia. A system exists that should not be disrupted."

"Don't try to play games with me!" I was thankful for the time I endured on my own and used it to practice harnessing my ability.

Before she could blink, I made stars pour out of my palms and over her entire body. I targeted specific ones to cling tighter to her neck, hands, and legs. I yanked her out of the cave and up into the air. She started to hyperventilate while being dangled from a nausea-inducing height.

"Stop! You don't know what you could do to me!"

"Yeah I do. I could turn you into the next Omar, nothing but a broken egg on the ground."

"What is it that you want?" the representative asked exasperatedly. "Zayika, you need to put me down!"

I didn't let her fall back to the dirt. I wanted her held high, to feel unsteady and out of reach from reality, similar to what I had to deal with. "Give me Anon."

"He was sent home with Amira. Us representatives, w-we didn't decide who came here."

I was smarter than to believe the way she was simplifying everything. "You're very bad at lying. You don't even try to act convincing. Do you think I'm unobservant?"

Her eyes started to search my face like she wanted me to tell her the right words to say. "No I don't."

"I know that you have powers too. You three representatives have to in order to remain alive. I watched you snap your fingers and make two people turn into a puff of dust. You are able to make them come and go, aren't you?"

She paused before answering. "No, I can't do that."

I tightened the current of stars around her throat and limbs. "Stop lying to me. If you lie again, I will kill you."

I kept my voice steady even though I was slightly worried. I didn't want to kill her because I knew I could truly be trapped forever without ever getting revenge and closure. I needed to play my cards right. *She won't call my bluff.*

"Zayika... I really don't want to die." Her eyes were welling up with tears as she tried to claw away from me. "Please show mercy!"

"Give me Anon. I will let you live if you do."

"Okay! I will bring him back!"

I was shocked. *I didn't think that would work so quickly.* I pulled her back over to the cave's entrance and let her go swiftly. After wincing and rolling side to side from falling on her tailbone, she put one of her hands towards the sky. With a regretful look on her face, the wind began to pick up. It was as if it was blowing in every direction all at once. My silver and purple hair was blowing over my face, obscuring my vision from seeing the full picture of what she was doing. For some reason it started to change. I watched as my hair turned entirely purple, the silver completely disappearing. I took my hand and held it out of the way to see what the representative did. There was a bright blue rain cloud that had formed and patterns of lightning began to spray out from underneath it.

"Be careful what you wish for, Zayika." the representative said as she got up and sprinted away.

I didn't say anything back. *She's just trying to scare me.* A chill scurried up my spine as I saw him. Anon emerged from the lightning and clouds and he fell into the ocean. I knew without a doubt that it was him, his large black wings no different than when I last saw them. Time seemed like it stood still as I watched his body plummet towards the waves. As a few moments passed, I closed my eyes and waited to hear the sound of him being coldly awoken from whatever peaceful dream he was in.

Three... two... one... Splash.

CHAPTER TWO: THROWING KNIVES

Nero

Present

The last thing I remembered was grabbing onto Zekiel's hair and forcing him into the unknown with me, something I chose to do without any doubt that I made the right call. He stole my last wing and the knee-jerk reaction I had was to make him pay. I floated around in a dark empty space with no idea where Zekiel was. No words could escape my mouth. *What type of place is this?* For a while I saw repetitive flashes of Saige's face imploding from the weapon I tossed. I targeted it at Zekiel because I knew she would take the knife for him. *She went invisible to step in front of the blade. How in love with someone do you have to be to sacrifice your life for them? Not sure what that's like.* The intensity of her selfless admiration for that man was undeniable. If I aimed at her I'm sure she would have used her abilities to outsmart me, resulting in a much greater challenge... but targeting the one person she couldn't get her eyes off of? Better chance of success.

I didn't feel too much remorse over her death since everything was part of the game after all. It was imperative to carefully strategize what actions to take, especially when and towards who. I planned to kill Saige all along in order to get her wish... and I did. Unfortunately, due to the asinine turn of events, Zekiel ended up getting the upper hand which he used to shred away the piece of me I needed to hold onto. *At least I was able to drag him into this hollow place too, it's what he deserves.*

There was no sign in the void to indicate if it was morning, night, or what time it had been at all. I kept drifting within a never-ending pit of trapped thoughts. *I have to get out of here.* What made it even worse was that I kept reliving the last few moments on the planet with Zekiel and Saige. As it replayed over and over again, I began to notice headache-inducing details about the event. *Zayika and Omar were there too.* Two members from the same Over Grounds faction. *Lousy teammates... they couldn't even take down Zekiel before he got to me.* I eventually was trapped in the void for so long that my thoughts started to contradict each other. *Well... I would have done the same thing if I was Zayika. I would have stood back and watched, too. Everyone has to fight for their own selves. Why would she risk her life to save me?* It was awful. *I can't really blame Omar for not helping, either, he couldn't kill a sand crab even if it would save his own life.* The thoughts were pouring in and my mindset kept shifting. *I can't blame Zekiel for taking my second wing since he was playing by the game's rules, right? Wouldn't I also have done the same thing if I were him?*

I became desperate to breathe in fresh air again as suffocation surrounded me. My stomach turned while I dwelled on a single memory, experiencing so much twisted emotion, but what also felt like nothing at the same time. Some sort of barrier seemed to block my voice from reaching the outside world. With strained vocal chords I yelled in an attempt to knock it down. Time was fleeing. *Opportunity is escaping.* Ridiculous thoughts wouldn't let me rest. I eventually broke down whatever was holding back my presence as words finally left my mouth, "Let me out of here! I'm begging whoever can help me! If you are listening and do this favor for me, I promise that I will help you with whatever you need!"

Light consumed the darkness. Even though my eyelids were closed, the newfound brightness scorched past them. *Did it work? Am I back on the planet?* Wind was picking up in circles at my feet and moving upwards. I clenched my teeth as I breathed in deeply. My ability was no use at that moment. I couldn't control the wind because it was controlling me. After what felt like a never-ending amount of being pulled back and forth and side to side... my body finally rested and felt at ease. Light started to fade and so did the thoughts that were previously paralyzing me. *I was right.* I was dropped off back into the planet's jungle right where the portal took me away. My confidence levels were rising. It was then that the conversation I had with Gebu became clearer than ever before. A transportation snap was apparently reversed and I got to discover what that truly meant.

I re-entered the game.

Hell yes.

Three Months Before

"Welcome to the planet, newcomer!" Gebu flew over to Nero, who was walking out from the morphing room. "Finally someone else is here! It's been lonely waiting for new members to arrive."

"Hi." Nero's eyes darted around the corridors and mysterious rooms he hadn't been in yet. "This is absolutely insane. I was so unsure of what would happen to me in that glass box."

"Likewise." he smiled. "I'm excited to have a friend here. It's difficult trying to interact with the representatives."

"Do you know what's going on? I have a lot of questions. Can you provide me with any answers?"

"I'll try to. Let me start from the beginning. I was minding my business on Earth conducting research at a waterfall when I was attacked by some crazy lunatic."

Nero's eyes lit up. "Did you say 'waterfall'?"

"Yep. I was harmed in broad daylight. Why? Did the same thing happen to you?" Gebu was hovering in the air and moved a bit closer. "You can trust me. Honestly. I have no one else to share your business with."

"Yeah. That sounds a lot like what happened to me."

"It seems you're taking all of this a lot better than I am, though. I'm not sure how many hours I've spent crying to myself. I'm so scared for the future."

Nero nodded uncomfortably. "We just have to figure out what's going on."

"It's surprising how calm you are staying... especially after being morphed. I've seen a few before you who didn't live through it."

"'Morphed'? What does that mean? You're referring to my wings, right?"

"Of course I am. There might be more to you than you think. You could have another ability."

"Really? That would be interesting. My shirt got torn up in the morphing process, but I don't think I even need to wear it anymore. These wings look pretty badass."

"They do. Have fun flying with them."

"How is it that you get around?" Nero asked with a smug look. "I see that you're floating."

"Um…" Gebu turned and showed him the small fragile green wings he was given.

Nero laughed and sarcastically replied, "Oh… Very cool."

"My name is Gebu. I forgot to properly introduce myself."

"I'm Nero." He flinched while moving his sore arm to shake his hand.

"Nice to meet you! Now we need to practice using our abilities and wait for everyone else to get here for the ceremony to start."

"What type of 'ceremony'?"

"We won't know for sure yet, but I have other insider information that I can let you in on. I'm the first person who came here so you might not want to miss it."

There was silence as Nero waited for him to continue.

"There's a guy here named Nathaniel, some dude who lives in a bunker eating packaged meals. He also has tons of canned water."

Nero listened lazily and after only one sentence went to find the closest mirror to look at himself. His new acquaintance wasn't discouraged by his reaction, though, and kept flying along to speak about details he felt should be shared.

"He showed me a stone outside by what is called the 'Land Dwellers' faction. It has information about this planet that we're on and why we are here. You know the name of our faction, right?"

"I was told that this is the 'Over Grounds' when I was taken to the glass boxes."

"Correct! We'll be the only group here with men that can get wings like ours."

"I'm not sure I'd call yours th—"

"But listen, Nero, we can't lose them. I was told that if we do then we get put in a wretched place. There's some type of void that consumes people who get their wings taken away."

Nero then actually began listening to Gebu's words. He turned to give him his undivided attention and leaned on the closest wall, bracing himself for any bad news.

"Seriously? What does that mean?"

"I don't know, but it sounds like we would be stuck there forever." He anxiously tapped his thumbs together while floating.

"That's intense."

"He said the only way someone could get out of there was if the transportation snap gets reversed."

Nero gave him a look of confusion. "I'm not following."

"We're fighting to get back to Earth, right? Well if someone successfully does that, but is for some reason called back here to the planet, the void will force out those who were let in."

"I'll keep that in mind."

"But no worries. I mean… Nathaniel did tell me that it's only once in a blue moon that something like that would even happen in the first place."

Present

Excitement coursed through my veins as I sauntered on the planet again, ready to see where everyone else was and fight my way to Earth. *There's more work for me to do.* Unfortunately, I no longer had my wings because of

Saylor and Zekiel. I was pissed even though I could see why they did that to me. I was about to earn Saige's wish, rightfully so, and tree hugger Zekiel sliced me open because of it. I wrestled with the bit of respect I had for him since he put up a fight... something that so many faction members were too scared to do.

It wasn't long after getting my bearings again until I realized how eerily quiet everything was. I didn't hear any action taking place. *How much time passed in that useless void? Damn it. Is everyone else gone? Is the game over?* I cracked my knuckles, aggravated at the lack of life around me. *My wind ability hasn't been stripped away too, has it?* I closed my eyes and began concentrating on using the power I was given. Air started to gradually build up speed and I used my palms to direct it where to go. *Good.* I then thought about the words the Oceanic Guardian representative said to us during the opening ceremony: "A new batch of people will be selected for each faction after this battle is over." *Well, screw me. Who knows how long that will take?*

I kicked some dirt into the air and groaned aloud. *What undeserving fool got to get back to Earth before I could? It better not have been some weakling like Omar. Hopefully it was someone who at least deserved it.* The best thing I could do was work on using my abilities again. I focused on manipulating the air and finding a fresh batch of throwing knives. *It wouldn't hurt to get back to practicing my aim.* I wasn't too far from the Land Dweller's faction grounds since the portal I was swept into opened in the jungle. To my advantage I found that their lofty treehouse contained leftover weapons in it—at least the ones that they didn't have to craft by using their hands. Eventually

I stumbled upon a box of blades I could use, so I took them with me and headed back outside.

As nightfall came, I heard a woman's voice that sounded like it was coming from the ocean. *Good. Someone else is here.* Something about her tone and vocal inflections seemed bizarrely familiar. With each step I tried to think of who it possibly could be. *Mae? Lyra?* I went over to her and almost dropped my handful of weapons when I realized who was speaking.

Zayika.

Seven Weeks Before

"Where did you both go? Get back here!" Nero called out after Saige and Zekiel as they ran away from him.

He panted heavily and watched the ground below as his blood fell onto it. The pain he was enduring was the worst he'd ever experienced. He winced and dropped the knife that he had used to slice Saylor's throat open. The other two Land Dwellers that Nero attacked were blown up into several small pieces. He twisted around in a circle to view the entire scene. *Why did he do this?* Saige and Zekiel parted ways as quickly as they could, even going invisible because of her morphed ability.

Nero felt an ache forming in his chest at the events that had unfolded and how quickly they escalated. He wasn't sure what to do for a little while but knew he needed to get back on track in order to survive. The opening ceremony on the planet was coming up soon which would reveal the purpose of the factions and what rules there would be. Nero spent many hours leading up to it preparing for combat. He harnessed his ability to use wind, fly, and throw knives until he had almost perfect precision in his aim and defense tactics.

Despite the surge of rising regret that he was feeling, he couldn't undo he had done, moving onwards and facing the wrath coming for him was inevitable. *Would he be reprimanded for fighting others before the trumpets rang out? Did he ruin his chance at going home based on a careless and vicious attack on the Land Dwellers?* Unanswered questions felt like poison to him. He walked back to the Over Ground's faction where his assigned dwelling place was located and took a rising platform up to the gates. While he was dipping his bloody hands into the first water bucket he could find, Gebu flew over to speak with him.

"Your wing! What happened? Are you okay?" Gebu's voice cracked.

"A mistake." Nero responded without making eye contact. "That's what happened."

"You fought someone? Already? But the game hasn't started ye—"

"I know. It shouldn't have happened the way it did."

"Y-you can't lose your other wing! Remember? You don't know what could be in store for you! Be more careful!"

"Gebu… I know." Nero clenched his jaw in pain as he tended to the wound on his back. "Thank you for caring, but you're really making this worse right now."

"Sorry. I'll try to calm down." Gebu responded quietly. "Let's go to Mae so she can heal you. It seems as though you've lost a lot of blood already."

"Alright. Yeah. That would be great if she could help."

"You're not acting like yourself, Nero. It seems like a switch has been flipped up there." Gebu pointed up at his head with a shaking finger. "While we're on our way can you please tell me what happened?"

"Yeah. I'll tell you the whole story." Nero sighed deeply. "It feels like I've just woken up."

Present

How is Zayika still here? The only reasonable conclusion would be that... she didn't win a wish. My guess was proved right as I discovered her on the shore pacing back and forth maniacally. She was wearing an outfit I'd never seen before, a bright white dress that shined under the starry night sky. I could hear her indistinctly whispering out loud to herself and was caught off guard by the way her voice sounded; it was strident and made me feel uneasy as I approached her. *It's surprising that she didn't make it to Earth. She is one of the few that were actually determined to get a ticket back. What went wrong?* Her hair looked different... and so did the way she was carrying herself.

"Zayika?" I asked loudly.

She turned around. "Are you serious right now? Nero, is that you?"

"It's your lucky day."

"No kidding. How are you back here? Where did you go?"

"I'm not sure how to describe the void I was forced into. It was only... emptiness."

Her eyes glanced at me and then over at the crashing waves. "No way. You're still alive?"

"I never died."

"How is this possible?"

"How are you still here?"

"Anon and Amira are the ones who got back to Earth, leaving me stuck here."

"I see. Where are the representatives?"

"Two are scattered all over Eunoia."

"They can be in several places at once?"

"No. I dismembered them."

Of course she did.

"What is 'Eunoia'?" I'd never heard that word before. *What could that mean?*

"It's the planet you're standing on. Somehow Amira cleverly figured that out." She rolled her eyes. "So, are you going to explain your side of things yet? Mine isn't that complicated. I want to know how you are in front of me right now."

"Did you by any chance, when taking the representatives apart, reverse who had been sent home? Bringing them back here?"

She furrowed her eyebrows and stepped close to my face. "How the hell would you know I did that?"

"Surprisingly enough, that is something Gebu told me a while ago when I first got here. Apparently there's a stone on this planet that contains information we can't fully comprehend."

"Awesome." Zayika pulled her hair over one side of her shoulders. "I'm not going to complain that you've been brought back. You're a good fighter. It will be nice to have you alongside me as I destroy Anon."

Wait... "What?"

"He's out in the water right now. He actually just got dropped off."

"If we fight him does that mean we get his wish? Does it even work anymore since he's already used it?"

"I don't know, he probably no longer has it, and I don't really care about that anymore. I just want to make him pay for what he did. Actions need to have consequences."

I don't fully understand her priorities.

"I'm not sure about you, Zayika, but I want to get back to where I should be."

"There's one representative left that I didn't kill, the one from our faction. She's somewhere roaming this planet right now. Maybe if you find her she can help you. If not, then have fun waiting for others to get here, if they are even Wish Carriers in the first place." she scoffed.

"Alright. I'll go look for her."

I knew that I couldn't get wrapped up in the delusions and schemes of others. My goal was clearer than ever before as I walked away on my own: *I have to get back to Earth.*

CHAPTER THREE: GUIDING LIGHT

Anon

Present

Suddenly I was in the ocean and my eyes sprang open as I flailed around in freezing water. I could hardly see anything while kicking my legs, which reminded me of trying to find a lighthouse on planet Eunoia. That was one of the worst experiences of my life. I was swimming in regret and memories that I tried to suppress. *I'm only dreaming. I have to wake up. This is another nightmare.* I closed and reopened my eyes, but nothing changed. Everything below me was pitch black. There was enough depth and darkness for something heinous to spring out from the ocean's trenches. With curled toes, an intrusive thought entered my mind: *What if that sea creature attacks me again? Is it down there?* My face was stinging and with a held breath I swam up to the surface. Through the tops of the waves, I could see stars glistening amongst several clouds in the sky. *What is going on?* Something below me began murmuring loudly. I recognized its pitch. *Hippo?* I launched myself upwards and got a deep breath of frigid air. I looked in every direction as my insides turned in horror. *Eunoia.*

My head felt warped as I realized just how doomed I really was. I searched until I could see land off in the distance. *The castle? The wheatfield? The jungle? No...* There was a silhouette of our Over Ground's broken castle and cluster of lengthy trees from the Land Dweller faction. I wasn't prepared to face the nightmare that kept me awake after I used my wish. It was extremely difficult to fall asleep back on Earth. Even going on with each day was a burden. I couldn't forget what Zayika said to me. Her promise was ingrained in my mind and I couldn't stand her for that. I had dreams of the blue trance night after night and would wake up springing out of bed to make sure Omar's blood wasn't still on my hands.

Anytime I wanted to move on with my life and forget about the planet, I couldn't because of the wings still branching out of my back. Facing my parents was nearly impossible. I knew I wouldn't be taken seriously and that they'd think I was lying and abandoned them. Even though my time on Earth was horrible, I'd always trade being there over the place where I was taken back to. Everything in my life changed against my will. *How am I here?* Unfortunately my question was answered by the one person who I never thought I'd face again.

"Anon! Did you miss me?" Zayika's piercing voice rang out. "Are you having trouble swimming out there?"

She came down to the sand from one of the white cliffsides and was surrounded by radiant stars.

"What is going on?" I screamed.

"Don't worry! I'll come save you!" she responded and began to glide over the water by traveling on rays of light that came out of her feet.

That's her ability... Before I could let out a breath, she was in front of me and put her hand out. *This is just another night terror. She is not really here.*

"I'm not awake." I tried to convince myself out loud.

"Aren't you going to be a gentleman and take my hand, Anon?" she asked with a menacing smile. "You aren't that good at swimming, so I figured I'd come rescue you. For old time's sake."

I rubbed my palms against my eyelids and frowned. "How is this happening?"

"Our story isn't over yet. Did you lose some of your memory from that fall? You don't remember what I told you the last time we saw each other?"

I shuddered at the reminder of her words: *"You will regret this Anon. I will never forget you. I promise that I will find a way to make you regret this."*

"I remember."

"Well take my hand. It's time for me to fulfill my promise." She rolled her eyes when I still didn't reach out. "Hurry up before one of the Oceanic Guardian creatures eat you. You and I have a lot of catching up to do, don't we?"

My hand tentatively met hers as she sped me along the tips of waves and back to the place that haunted me. Eunoia. The jungle was overgrown and withering, the floating castle still in ruins, and the ocean water looked like ink. *I wonder if there have been more earthquakes?* The rubble off to my right which belonged to my previous faction caught my attention. One of the memories that plagued me back on Earth was the image of Omar's head cracked open on my lap. There was no end to the amount of blood that kept coming out of him. I was in a blue trance. The planet was destroyed, and oddly enough it seemed as though it was going to become what I saw in that moment very soon as we both reached the shore.

"What are you thinking about?" Zayika asked me. "No hug? You're not even going to thank me for saving you again?"

"Why am I here? Has a new fight started? Where are all of the faction members?"

She guffawed at my words. "You wish. I just ran into Nero... but no, Anon, it's nothing like that."

"He's alive? Wait, what?" I was stunned. "What's going on?"

"I'm getting my revenge." Her boots made her even taller as she looked down at me with distaste.

I stepped backwards from her as she smirked and began tapping her fingers against one another. I bit my lip nervously and tried to brace myself for whatever she was going to throw my way.

"Why did you have to bring me back? You should have just fought your way to Earth like I did. You wanted the reward without taking the risk, Zayika, and you're weak because of tha—"

A huge amount of air left my lungs in an instant. Traveling at the speed of light, she placed her hand against my chest and released a cluster of shaking stars. My throat was burning as I struggled to breathe.

"Don't ever call me that again. You don't know what I'm capable of." Zayika shoved me backwards with full force, finally releasing me out of her hold.

I hit the sand and gasped with a speechless expression. Every fear I had since returning to Earth was becoming a reality. "Please..." I started to say.

"'Please' what? Please stop?" She shrugged. "That word means nothing. I used it when I asked for you and Amira to take me home and neither of you gave a damn."

Zayika began to light up again, making me partially cover my eyes. She was so agonizingly bright. I tensed up every muscle with certainty that I was about to die. My heart was heavy with sorrow. I wanted so badly to have never been a part of Eunoia. I wished I had never met Zayika and the storm cloud she brought with her everywhere that rained down on others. I was ready to give up and accept the fate of having my entire life lost at the touch of her hands. Then... something happened. There was another beaming glow, but it wasn't coming from her. Hippo was rising from the ocean with her giant orb. I felt my heart skip a beat once I saw who was there too.

"Amira?" Zayika clenched her fists.

I could do nothing but smile.

Six Weeks Before

Amira and Anon survived planet Eunoia's challenge and used their wishes to get back to Earth after destroying the mysterious waterfall. They left Zayika to fend for herself and always felt plagued by their decision. When the representative brought on the burst of light to bring them home, they were taken to a faraway beach on Earth. It was nighttime when they returned and no one else could be seen. The two had been knocked out when transported and Anon was the first to wake up. He pulled his face away from the wet sand and grains were stuck to his face. After brushing them off, he looked to see where he was as small waves crashed over his body. Up ahead he saw the beach parking lot and a line of closed merchandise shops. There was also a shining lighthouse on top of a large rock pile.

He saw Amira laying down beside him and that the orange tail was still where her legs should have been. The sight of this prompted him to frantically check his back and he discovered that his wings were still attached. Confused, he sprung up and tried to pull them off. He winced at how tight the skin was where the wings had sprouted out from. *Why did he not wish for his body to be unmorphed?* He went to Amira and lightly patted her shoulder.

"Hey." Anon spoke. "We're on Earth."

She awoke suddenly and rolled over to see what was going on. "Anon?"

"Yeah, it's me. Look where we are."

The streetlights from the beach's entrance gave off a soft glow over the ocean and stretches of sand on either side of them.

"It actually happened!" Her smile wasn't met with one by him. "What's wrong?"

"We're still morphed."

Amira looked down and saw that it was her tail moving, not legs. "I didn't even realize…" She inspected him closely. "Wow, I didn't see your wings in the dark for a second there."

He started to panic. "I don't know what we're going to do. We're going to be like this forever. What if we can't get back to our old selves? We aren't going to be accepted here! There's no way we will ever live a normal life!"

"Shh." She placed her hand on top of his. "We can find a way around this. We just have to stay close to one another as we've already done."

Anon nodded and placed his hand on hers. "Alright."

Present

"What is going on?" Amira called out to us while on top of Hippo's head. "How am I back here?"

"Amira!" I stood up and started waving my arms.

"I might as well have fun with this." Zayika huffed air out of her nose.

Hippo looked as frightening as when I last saw her. Her black eyes reflected the sky's stars like gigantic polished marbles. The anglerfish appeared to be bigger than any whale from Earth and had teeth which were pointy and sharp enough to cut through anything. *Thankfully she will never attack me.* The noises she made were borderline deafening as they demanded everyone's attention and rattled the land and water surrounding us relentlessly. Most of her cries sounded as if they had the intent to intimidate others if they were a threat to Amira or me, but in this case the wails from her gaping mouth seemed joyful, telling us in her own way how excited she was to fight alongside us again.

Amira's legs were replaced with her orange tail when she also fell down into the ocean. Hippo had risen from the depths of the water to assist her in getting over to where we stood. She threw her hands up in a surprised gesture. "Anon!" She seemed at ease when noticing me, but then was back on edge at the realization of who was by my side. "I'm not dreaming, am I?" she said loudly.

"Unfortunately we aren't." I responded and flew up into the air shakily while rediscovering the feeling of flying. I felt uncomfortable at first, but my instincts kicked in quickly. "I'm right here. Stay by me." I reached down to take Amira off of Hippo and held her in my arms. We flew over to the sand and I laid her down softly so that she could return to her unmorphed state.

"You are both delusional if you think this is some sort of reunion party." Zayika got in between us. "I only asked for Anon."

"Well, we left together." Amira responded as she watched glossy scales slough themselves off her wet skin.

I promptly walked past Zayika and back over to Amira's side. "We're sort of a two for one deal."

"I guess I should have figured that out." Zayika looked aggravated as she turned away from us and stared at the cliffs, drifting away in thought.

Although I was glad to see Amira, who brought me peace, I was upset that she had been thrown into this with me. *Nothing good can come from this. Zayika will not act lightly on the remnants of her dark, twisted mind.*

Zayika looked at Amira and me with curious eyes. "I want to get this over with, you know, my revenge. Admittedly it's pretty interesting talking to you both again... but I should've started fighting you two by now. Are you ready to see what I can do?"

Her hands flashed with light and strands of her purple hair swiftly stood up in the wind. Zayika's green eyes locked onto me first. I gave a fake half-smile. *I don't want to attack her.* Internally, I battled against pursuing the logical approach to the events unfolding before me. *But I have to fight.* I let my arms fill with lightning again. I forgot how bad the sting that it brought was, which made me glance down to make sure my arms were still intact. I checked on Amira before flying upwards. "Are you okay?"

"You know I can handle myself." She smiled.

I was never sure how she seemed to handle conflict so well. Deep down I knew that she was also worried but was better at covering it up.

"Anon... you don't have to try to act so tough." Zayika broke the tension in the air. "I remember the first time you killed Nathaniel and you went crying to Omar about it."

Don't bring that up. "You don't know what you're talking about."

"I'll catch you up since you have a bad case of selective memory. You wanted to be the leader. That failed, of course, but in your attempts to help the rest of us you killed Nathaniel—that antisocial hermit from the bunker." Zayika looked at Amira and laughed. "Then after doing so you went and cried into your pillow over the death of a man you didn't even know. If you kill me, Anon, you will be broken all over again. Especially since at one point you believed that I was your friend."

She was both right and wrong. I at one point did want to lead the group that I met on the starting hills, though over time I realized that I was misconstruing what my goal should have been all along. I discovered the type of person Zayika really was. People believed that there was a kind side to her. I also fell for the mask of deception that made it seem as though her vileness was a method of compensation to cover up hidden pain. No. There was never another side to her, it was always in plain sight without shame. She saved my life in the past. I discovered that the reason behind this was only to have another person willing to pay her back and feel as though they owed her something. She was never the type to actually care for anybody else. Zayika noticed how I was trembling and showed how overjoyed that made her with a malicious smirk.

Frustration boiled inside of me. "If you're going to attack us then just do it already."

"Bold talk coming from you!" she shrieked and sent a ray of stars towards me before I could react.

It hit me like a pan of boiling hot water. I screamed and tried to shoot a bolt of lightning at her, but for some reason it bounced back at me instead. Every vein within my body felt as though a flame-filled match had been taken to it. All I felt was searing pain and grabbed both of my forearms. *What has she done?*

"See Anon? I told you that I could deal damage with my ability!"

Amira got up and made her way over to Zayika. "You should not have done that." She grabbed her arm and twisted it roughly, a loud crunching pop emerged as it went out of the socket.

"Ah. This is all you've got, Amira?" Zayika covered herself in her stars again and the contorted arm went back to normal. "That barely hurt me. Wow, I guess without your rotten fish you really can't do anything. You're almost on Omar's level of worthlessness."

Zayika's goal was to get under our skin... and she was succeeding. To our disadvantage, her words were as razor-edged as the powers she was given. *She really can heal herself.* I felt a rush of panic fall over me as I connected together the pieces of how capable she was of raining down hell. Zayika truly was unstoppable. It was clear to us in the past that the morphing process was similar to the lottery. Purely based on luck. Some people were killed right away when it happened to them, and others were given great abilities with physical drawbacks, but she had won it all. *She can protect herself and simultaneously do the worst to everyone around her.*

"Why do you look so scared, Anon?" She skipped towards where I was hovering in distress. "You are terrified! Why are you acting so serious? What happened to you? Weren't you the jokester? You know, the one dishing out all the irrelevant pop culture references and bad puns or whatever?"

"Just… stop." I felt sick.

"Aw, let me guess, someone stole your innocence?" Zayika smiled with her mocking tone.

"That's enough." Amira looked excited for what she was about to say next. "Hippo, attack."

Those two words were all that was needed for the colossal anglerfish to make her presence distinctly known again. The familiar sound of her rushing our way filled the air. Her mouth was wide open, ready to devour whoever she needed to. The booming noises she made sounded unnerving as I put my hands up to my ears. Water fell down from the top of her head as she got closer and started to devour a part of the shore with extreme vigor.

"Wow! I'm so scared!" Zayika stated sarcastically.

Amira stood near her fish confidently as it charged ahead. I flew up a bit higher to stay out of the way, still feeling the aftermath of discomfort from Zayika's ability colliding against mine. Hippo was a force of nature that was not to be reckoned with, but Zayika was prepared and overjoyed to do just that. She sent a rippling beam of stars directly into the anglerfish's mouth that hit the back of her throat. Another roar shook the ground, trees, and even heavy rocks surrounding us. Hippo's humongous pair of eyes creepily darted around and started spinning in circles.

"What's happening?" Amira was growing concerned. "Did you hurt her?"

She must be stunned. "We have to go right now!" I shouted.

I immediately swooped down and picked up Amira while Zayika was temporarily distracted by Hippo's odd behavior. She held onto me tightly as she looked at her fighting companion sitting still in what was probably very painful shock.

"What are we going to do, Anon?"

"We have to hide."

CHAPTER FOUR: DEPTH OF FIELD

Amira

Present

The night was filled with threats and malice which made it hard to anticipate what was waiting for us at each corner, but our priorities were clear. *Find a way to win against Zayika. Get back to Earth. Survive.* She was the most vindictive and selfish person I'd met. A miserable storm followed her around everywhere and she wasn't pleased until her hands forced others to suffer too. I refused to let the situation we were in get the best of me. *Stay confident and strong. We have to use our minds in order to outsmart her. Focus on what matters.* Hardly any time had passed since being brought to Eunoia and I already missed so many things about Earth. It was unbelievable to be able to see my family again and try to explain to everyone who knew me there why I was gone for so long.

I was grateful to have Anon by my side. We remained close to one another and I tried to comfort him when he would have nightmares of the past we endured. I was asleep in my home when the tragedy started. First there was the sensation of falling, and then I was descending into the ocean at an alarming pace. For a few minutes it felt like every bone in my body had shattered upon impact with the waves. I woke up but was no longer in my bed. Right away I knew where I was as a tail reappeared over my legs. I started swimming to go to the shore but was assisted in doing so by the sea creature I named Hippo. The giant anglerfish rose from the waters below and surprised me as I was lifted on top of her head. Her hanging orb lit the way as a guiding light while we both went over to the shore. *Is that Anon up ahead?* I was overwhelmingly relieved to see that he was also alive and grateful that I had Hippo to accompany me again, but I was also furious at Zayika for stripping away our freedom.

A feeling told me that something very awful was going to happen to some of us on the planet, and my heart was set on making sure it wouldn't be Anon or me. I always felt a connection to him ever since we first met at the hills on Eunoia near the ocean when he caught my attention. He seemed curious and anxious to do outrageous things with the right intentions. I had a deep-rooted desire to accompany him in solving the problems laid before us. His dream to be a leader was charming, and his shortcomings at doing so made it a bit amusing at times too. There were flaws to him that he couldn't hide. I also had my own, but I was better at disguising them. *We have to stay strong in our decision to leave Zayika. Everyone has to learn at some point that life is not fair, and every person is responsible for getting themselves over it.*

There were limited places in Eunoia that allowed us to stay under the radar. Zayika's blinding stars and awareness made it seemingly impossible to get away from her for long. Anon and I fled away from her presence, but I knew that our time was limited; she would be back soon. We were in dire need of a real plan. Anon needed stability and I tried to provide it to him, though in some moments it was more difficult to do so than in others. We ran away to hide from the fight at the ocean, but I knew we couldn't pretend that our lives weren't on the line.

"Zayika is literally insane!" Anon's voice was shaking as he flew down to the ground behind a large cluster of vines near the Land Dweller's faction. "We have to take action!"

"What do you think we should do?" I asked him.

"Well... we are going to have to find the representatives and talk to them. I'm sure they can figure something out. We can probably be sent back to Earth just as we were before." His brown eyes met mine with a glint of hopefulness. "We'll be okay."

"Yeah. I hope so." I replied, trying to not sound cynical.

"What do you mean you 'hope'? We have to be certain. We will be okay." Anon's voice was a bit stern.

I sighed. "That's what I meant to say."

He rubbed both sweaty hands against his pants and gave a half smile. "Sorry for being short with you. It's just... Amira... I'm scared. I don't want to admit it, but I truthfully never thought that we'd come back here. I would have never guessed we would have to face Zayika again. It's horrifying having to look back on previous decisions and answer so many questions about them, memories that I never wanted to revisit."

"I know. It's okay to be scared, we just have to make sure that we don't run with our fear to the point of it getting us killed. We have to kill our fear."

"Let's change the subject." he suggested.

I sat against a large tree trunk and he got down next to me, shuffling slightly to get comfortable despite having wings stemming out from his back. "This time we should ask them if we can have our abilities removed before we get home."

"We were so caught up in the moment, but it's completely unfair how they sent us back in our morphed state without bringing that mistake to our attention. How do they expect us to function in society? You grow a tail and I, well, it's sort of hard to miss. These wings make me look like I'm wearing a costume. The lightning is also not the best conversation starter."

The two of us were trying to make everything seem much less serious than it really was. Being back on Earth with Anon while morphed was horrifying. Thankfully we had each other and made sure we were safe, but there was no possibility of living a relaxing life.

"How are you doing?" I examined his skin. "Did you see this? Does it hurt?"

"What?" he asked, and his eyes followed my gaze.

The patterns of lightning on his arms were still there, which was something I'd never seen before. When he was done using his power, they would always go away, but this time it seemed as though he had been scarred when Zayika blocked his attack. *He was struck by his own lightning.* There were many light red scars in the shapes of branches all over both arms, his chest, and traveling up his neck.

"I'm not too surprised this happened. When my lightning collided against those stars… it was awful… but I'm feeling better. I guess I know what it feels like to be hit with my ability. I'm feeling pretty bad for those I've done this to in the past now." He ran a fingertip over them, noticing how they were slightly raised. "I think it looks cool, honestly. Guess I don't have to get a tattoo now."

I chuckled. "You were serious about that?"

"Yeah, I really wanted one. We would've been at that tattoo parlor already if it wasn't for Zayika, you know, ruining our lives. I guess she wasn't joking about all of that."

"You could see in her eyes how serious she was."

"That's why I tried my best to not look into them. I was scared that if I did… I would never escape." He placed his arm comfortably around me. "So Amira, what's it like not being in the water?"

"It's a nice change not having to stay so close, which is the only good thing that came out of being taken home. If I was still stuck near it, I'm not sure what I would do. It's just a shame that I continuously get a tail forced upon me if I go under at all."

"You're a real life mermaid." Anon started to laugh.

"Why are you laughing? What's funny?"

"I'm just remembering something Gebu said to me a while ago when I was talking about you to him and Omar."

"What is it that he said?"

"He asked if you sang 'siren songs' to me and I told him no." Anon ran his free hand through his hair and sighed.

"What made him ask that? Besides the obvious mermaid joke. Why would he think I'd sing to you?"

"Ah, it's nothing. He just thought there was something going on between us. You know… romantically."

We sat and listened to the sound of wind whirring through the trees above us. It felt as though we were the only two people on the planet, even though we knew that we weren't. It was an odd feeling to be back on Eunoia without many others nearby fighting in their designated factions. No cries for help, groups fighting, or trumpets sounding. I enjoyed Anon's company and embrace. I was comfortable and wanted to remain hopeful for many more moments in our future feeling that way.

"What made him think that?" I looked at him and our eyes met.

"Oh, because we'd talk often. I guess others took notice when we would meet by the ocean. That and how we didn't attack one another even though we were from different factions."

"Well, what did you say to him?"

"I told him that we were just friends."

"We 'were'? Are we still now?"

Anon's lips crept into a wide smile. "I'm so confused by your wording, I don't know how to answer."

We both started laughing.

"Here. Let me sing you a siren song." I gently moved Anon's arm away from behind me.

While carefully holding onto his wings, I motioned for him to get closer and fall down onto my lap. He slowly laid down on top of me and became more relaxed while watching the sky through swinging leaves.

"You're really going to serenade me?" he asked. I could tell he was trying to not look too excited.

"Yeah."

"Why is that?" I saw him look up at my lips and then into my eyes.

"To enjoy the moment before we risk our lives to find a representative." I put my hand on the top of his head.

"We will be okay, Anon. I'm glad you've stuck by me through all of this."

"Are you kidding? I'm glad that you have stuck by me."

I took a short moment to remember the lyrics and began the song's melody as a subtle hum and then sang to him as he closed his eyes. The clouds were watching us and each gust of wind felt like the planet was somehow letting out a deep breath of air. *We'll get through this. Everything has led up to this moment for a reason.* I put my right palm against the side of his face and he leaned onto it. *I wish my camera was here right now.*

Eunoia had never felt so peaceful before.

Six Weeks Before

Amira and Anon were relieved to be back on Earth, but they had encountered many obstacles for them to overcome and adjust to. The employee behind one of the beach's gift shop counters lent them extra clothes to wear free of charge once the morning arrived. After leaving the beach they walked along the sidewalk and waved their arms into the air, hoping to catch a taxi ride to one of their homes.

"Do you still feel okay?" Anon looked at Amira's legs. "You seem to be walking steadily."

"Yeah I'm okay." Her smile was radiant when she answered. "My skin feels a lot different. I don't think I need to run to the water anytime soon."

Anon smiled back. "I'm glad to hear it. I really hope that doesn't change."

"I'm sorry about your wings... that you still have them."

"It's okay." He bit his lip softly and shrugged.

"What do you think about all of the looks you're getting?"

Anytime someone drove or walked past the two, they gave Anon a startled or puzzled glance. Passersby were incredibly intrigued and awfully curious to know why they were there.

"I think I'll get used to being stared at eventually. That cashier was extremely confused. I could tell he was holding back from asking me why I look the way I do."

Amira took Anon's hand in hers. "We'll figure something out, okay?"

He took a heavy breath and thought carefully about the words he spoke next. "I'm not sure what my parents are going to say about all of this. I'm not even sure which one to visit first. How do we explain anything? Being gone for so long? They're going to think I left them in the dark and that I'm hiding things."

"I'm sure they will understand. Whose house are we closer to from here? I've never been to this beach before."

"Mine are a bit far. We'll have to ask the taxi driver for a GPS to determine the distance from yours." Anon turned his head to look at her.

When a taxi finally stopped, the two explained upfront that they didn't have money with them. The driver agreed with Amira's request to be paid upon arrival at her parent's house, which they discovered was the closest one to where they were located. The drive was bittersweet. Comforting music played through the speakers as they both had flashbacks of everything that happened on Eunoia. Amira tiredly put her head down on Anon's shoulder and was about to drift into a deep sleep until the stranger in the front seat spoke.

"So, dude, what's with the wings? You know it's not even close to being the end of October... right?"

Anon quickly thought of an excuse. "I'm an artist. I filmed a new music video."

Amira gave a half-smile to keep from bursting into a roar of laughter.

"Wow. Really?" The driver was buying it. "What kind of music do you perform?"

"Umm... a mix of many genres."

Anon looked out of the window, bouncing his legs up and down while Amira let out a laugh, despite her best attempts not to.

"He's very talented." She tried to play along.

The driver nodded his head and redirected his full attention to the road. "Awesome."

The two in the backseat hid their smiles as the taxi carried them along several twisting roads and crowded traffic.

"Nice answer." Amira whispered in Anon's ear.

Present

My song was finished and Anon gave me a soft round of applause. "That was much needed. Thank you. Mermaids really do have the most beautiful voices."

"You're welcome."

"That and... you are beautiful, too."

Did I hear him right?

"Thank you Anon." I felt myself blushing. "Um, well, remember you said that you're a musical artist yourself. I still have yet to get a glimpse of your vast talent in performing 'many' genres."

"We will save that for another day." He got up, smiling, and put his hand out to help me stand. "I don't want to face Zayika's wrath, I really don't, but it seems that we have no other choice."

"If I had known we would be back here so soon, I would've tried to bring a camera with me." I dusted myself off. "Maybe then people on Earth would believe that this is a real place if we could show them our story."

"They'd probably say it's photoshopped." Anon chuckled. "I'm just being honest."

Then, in the distance, we heard what sounded like something snapping underneath someone's feet. We looked at each other in confusion and silently agreed to go see who it was. Anon made sure his arms were out in front of him, ready to attack if needed. I was close by with heightened senses and observed the jungle. There were some parts of the planet I hadn't seen before. It was very intriguing to find out that it was where the Land Dwellers came from. I finally got to see their terrain.

"This has to be some sort of joke." the person nearby said. "What kind of dream is this?"

We followed the direction of where his voice was coming from, careful to make sure we wouldn't fall into some sort of trap placed by Zayika.

He continued, "No way. Oh no... this can't be real." sounding as if he was looking at something awful.

"Stay right here." Anon whispered to me. "I'm going to see who this is. What if it's the Land Dweller representative?"

"It doesn't sound like him." I replied. "But okay, I'll wait. Be careful."

Who is out there? This can't be someone new to the planet... I destroyed the waterfall. I made sure that no one could be brought here again, right? I realized something. *Should I have asked for the planet to be destroyed as a whole... not just the waterfall? What if I did not think my wish through?*

I watched as Anon stepped slowly ahead. He tried to not make any sudden movements or sounds that would startle the person we were trying to observe. I truly had no idea who could be at the faction with us. Zayika was the only other person on the planet when we left, besides the three representatives. I put my hand up to my forehead as I tried to think of who it might be. *Zekiel disappeared... Saige and Omar died... there was no one else left over from our group. No other men... at least that I know of.* Out of nowhere it suddenly hit me. *Someone new has been taken to Eunoia to be morphed!* I believed that the planet called someone unknown to fight and participate in the next game of wishes. I wanted to call out after Anon, but he had already gotten very close to whoever was there.

"Put your hands up!" he was told.

"Woah! I'm not going to hurt you!" Anon exclaimed.

I got nearer so that I could see the exchange taking place.

"There's a dead person right here. You see this? A woman." the stranger informed him. "Do you know anything about this?"

I was unsure of who it was at first, but I could see the rotting body he was referring to. Recollections of previous crime scenes started to intrude my thoughts as I tried to not think about them. *Stay focused...* I saw a different intrusive flash each time I blinked for a little while. *Something is wrong.* I looked behind me to make sure no one was stalking us. Thankfully, I saw no silhouettes or other footprints and redirected my attention up ahead.

"There's a blade sticking out where her face should have been! Come on, you need to explain yourself. I haven't seen anyone else around here so why don't you tell me what's going on?"

Anon stopped walking. "I wasn't involved in that woman's death. I promise. I'm not here to hurt you, just trying to understand where you came from."

"Why do you have wings on your back? Are those real?"

"Yes, they're real."

"Prove it."

Anon leapt into the air and hovered above him. "You don't know where you are, do you? How did you get here?"

As the man watched Anon, he noticed the patterns of lightning scars covering his skin.

With furrowed eyebrows, he replied, "I was sleeping like every other night. When I woke up from dreaming, I was on a big hill. I'm pretty sure I'm still asleep. This cannot be real. You are not real."

"Welcome to Eunoia. This place is the gift that keeps on giving." Anon sparked blue and white fluorescent lightning with his right arm in front of his chest. "I managed to escape it but have just been brought back. You too can be its own personal boomerang."

"What in the world are you even talking about?" He blinked rapidly. "I now know for sure that I'm dreaming. That's not possible. You do not have lightning in your arms."

Anon fired off a very small bolt in the opposite direction and it crashed into a lumpy boulder. "You aren't dreaming. Give it some time and you'll be up to speed shortly."

If only that bolt hit Zayika. She's probably watching us right now as we speak... or trying to find the pieces of her mind that she lost when we left her here.

"Don't be frightened." I spoke with leaden steps.

"Who are you guys?" He put his hands into his pockets and looked at the jungle in awe. "I've never been in a place like this before. Do you both know what's going on?"

I grabbed Anon's hand as he went to stand next to me. "I'm Amira and this is Anon. You're not on Earth anymore, this is Eunoia."

A blaring sound of some type of voltage split through the air. There were fragments of Zayika's voice, revealing her presence to us that was drawing closer. *We need to do something. We can't wait around for her to create more havoc.* I was worried about what she would do to bring us misery but was partly more interested in giving her a taste of the lethal medicine she wanted forced down our throats. *Make a plan. Anon can't keep changing the topic that we have to address.* I wanted to know more about the person who we stumbled upon. He seemed to be taking the news of Eunoia well and was open-minded about adapting. *We have to convince him that we are not who he needs to resist. He could be helpful in getting rid of Zayika and we'll need all the help we can get in order to do that.*

"We don't have long to talk." Anon told him. "We'll explain more once we get under some cover, so keep your voice down and stay close by. There's somewhere that we can go for now until she finds us."

"Who are you talking about?" the man asked.

"Someone who I guarantee you will regret ever meeting."

I can't say I disagree with him.

The man followed us into the Land Dweller's quarters. The building was ominous and numbingly cold as we went through their corridors and past the cracking wooden door frames. Their packages of food and tubs of water were empty, handles for weapons were lying around, and the sounds of our steps traveled throughout each hallway. Vines were growing inside on the walls and there were sizable branches supporting the ceiling like pillars, making it appear to be a treehouse. It was vastly different compared to the underwater castle that my faction used for morphing and regrouping. Every once in a while we would see a different sea creature swim by our windows that Hippo was happy to get rid of for us, but there wasn't anything like that on the enemy grounds. *Do any of the Land Dwellers even get fighting companions? Am I the only one from the thirty who was assigned one?* It was a letdown to not have my camera. There were so many unique sights that I wanted to document and create an album of. *I wonder what the castle in the sky is like? Maybe, before we leave, I can convince Anon to fly me up there to see it. I bet it's incredible.* We stumbled upon a room with stone beds in each corner stained by blood and partly fractured in places. *This must be where people get morphed, but where do the bodies of those who did not survive go? The stone didn't mention that... I haven't seen any cemeteries here.*

"So... can we talk about what's going on?" the stranger broke the silence. "I'm sorry, I just have a lot of questions."

"We do too, but we will try to answer whatever you throw at us." Anon sat on one of the beds and swung his feet back and forth. "What is your name?"

"Jameson."

"Nice to meet you. You are now in a dreamworld. This planet brought us here a while ago to fight others that were placed into different factions."

I chimed in to help explain. "There were three. Land Dwellers, Oceanic Guardians, and the Over Grounds. People were morphed when they arrived after being sought out and chosen by faction members. We were forced into their settlements against our will and underwent... unsettling transformations that have left us not entirely human anymore."

"I don't understand." He started to pace around in the room between Anon and me. "Why?"

I have to mention the engravings. "We'll never be completely sure, but there was a stone that was destroyed by a storm here and it told of magical beings called 'Wish Carriers' who were those truly destined to go back to Earth."

Jameson stopped in his tracks. "'Wish Carriers'? I've never heard that before. What does that mean? How are they able to get back home?"

"It means that the person is extremely valuable. They possess the key that everyone wants to get their hands on. This key is called a 'wish'. It can be stolen from them, or they can work together to share and compromise with it. One of the representatives assigned to the Over Grounds faction is able to let those that have a wish return to Earth."

"What type of dream were you having before you arrived here? Did you feel any pain?" Anon asked him.

"Yeah... oddly enough. I just assumed it was a night terror mixed with paranoia of some sort."

Anon looked at me with intrigue. We kept exchanging glances while Jameson grew disoriented.

"What are you two talking about?" He tilted his head. "I can tell that you're like, telepathically discussing something."

"Were you hurting in your dream?" I asked. "Did you feel any pain at all? Even slight discomfort?"

"Yes."

The room was so quiet that you could hear a needle hit the dirt layered floor.

"Where was the pain localized in your dream?" Anon was biting his lip again.

He's thinking exactly what I am, I just know it. This man is a Wish Carrier too.

He was hesitant to answer at first. "It was the—"

Zayika's voice interrupted our conversation. The tree-like building we were in rattled like it was going to collapse in on itself as she began to flood almost every room with purple whirling stars. My face started dripping sweat from the sudden heat and I used my shirt to soak up most of it. Her voice cut through the atmosphere like a serrated knife as she glided over to us and put both her hands on the doorway with a forceful clasp. Her long nails clicked against the walls as she looked around for a moment. *This can't go well. I have no way of fighting her if I'm not near Hippo… why does this place have to be so wiped clean of everything?*

"What are you both doing? Anon, it's charming how you think that you can hide from me. Have you ever been told that you're indescribably naive?" Zayika's attention locked onto our new acquaintance. "Looks like the planet brought us someone new to have fun with. I've never seen you before. Who are you?"

"I'm Jameson." He stepped towards her. "It's nice to meet you. Nice hair."

"Thanks, it has a mind of its own." she responded. "Are you a problem maker or a problem solver?"

Anon was annoyed, "Oh, come on Zay—"

"I'd like to believe that I am the latter." Jameson gave her a smile.

As he reached out to shake her hand, Anon couldn't refrain from yelling. "No! Don't touch her! You'll get hurt!" He jumped up and flew in front of them. "She's a poisonous person!"

"No I'm not. But if I was, Anon, how would you know? It takes one to know one." She rolled her eyes and shook her head in frustration. "Looks like you're the one with issues here."

Jameson put his hands up slowly. "What is going on?"

Zayika shrugged. "Nothing. I think he's just upset that all of the attention won't be on him for once—that or he's worried there is competition with you here." she looked at me, her tone laced with mockery. "Don't worry, Anon, I'm pretty sure Amira only has eyes for you—for some reason that the rest of us will never know."

"Give it a rest." Anon replied to the hit of his self-esteem.

Zayika walked closer to Jameson and looked up at his face. "You're very tall. Hey Anon, do you remember what the other fighters said about Zekiel at that cave? They mentioned how his build could come in handy. I'd like to see you two fight, honestly, that would be some entertainment I'm in need of." She looked over his arms for a sign of any possible abilities. "What faction do you belong to?"

"Not sure. This all just keeps getting weirder." He laughed a bit in between each word.

"Let's find out what you can do." She grinned and took his arm in her hand.

"What are you doing?" I asked her. "Don't make a game out of this."

"That's the point of everything. You all should have known that since the opening ceremony took place." Zayika didn't care, of course, about anyone else's concerns. "So, Jameson… we need to find out what you're capable of and if you've been appointed to a faction by the planet. Do you trust me?" She beamed with wonder.

I was in utter disbelief when he nodded and let her lead him over to one of the stone slabs.

Anon came up to me and whispered in my ear, "I hate when people fall for her obvious antics."

"I know." I whispered back. "But this guy can make his own decisions. We're lucky enough right now that Zayika is keeping things civil."

"That won't last long though, she loves unnecessary theatrics. If anything, she just wants to get him on her side or… draw out time before she really tries to kill us."

Jameson sat down and Zayika stood by his side with enjoyment. "Now we wait." she said. "Let's see if you also get changed. I think you will, there's definitely potential within you."

"Seems like you're capable of a lot yourself." he told her.

"What should we do?" Anon asked me while the other two kept complimenting each other.

I hope he doesn't turn against us or get the same morphing results as Zayika.

"We can't just run away over and over again or get distracted. We're going to have to defeat her." I said firmly.

"How?" I could hear his throat becoming dry.

It didn't take long for me to put the pieces together. "We need Jameson on our side with his wish. He's definitely a Carrier."

CHAPTER FIVE: REM SLEEP

Jameson

Present

Why was I brought here? In a short amount of time I met three others who were not fully human in the strangest place I'd ever seen. I ventured along steep and seemingly never-ending hills, through wheat fields so high that I couldn't see anything past them, and a jungle which felt like its narrowly tangled pathways closed in on themselves more with each step. I initially thought that everything was a dream, but it didn't take long for me to realize how real everything was before me. I was taken somewhere that I never knew existed. *How is any of this possible?* Every unnatural color was so vivid and rain clouds that looked like waves cascaded above me. *A storm is approaching.* There were faint rumbles of thunder that made themselves known and it sounded like there were voices talking down to me and I couldn't make out what they were saying.

Before I knew it, my exploration took a darker turn. I came across a woman's corpse lying amongst the vines with a knife sticking out of her face. *Stay calm.* I could sense danger, but I had to stay level-headed in order to escape it. I met a man named Anon whose arms looked like he had dipped them inside of the sky and a piece of it remained with him. The same could be said for Zayika with her long purple hair which fell past her shoulders. The two were clearly at war against the other. Another woman who had the name Amira was also with us. She was calm with a strong demeanor and clearly shared an unwavering bond with Anon.

I was unsure of whose words to believe and take direction from, but something about Zayika was distractingly mesmerizing. There was a type of unearthly beauty to her that was impossible to not notice. *She is outwardly stunning, but what is her mind like?* She was a woman who exuded power and knew that she had it. Something about the way she walked around told me so much about her without a word having to escape her mouth.

We came across a plant-like structure in the middle of the jungle and they tried to explain what was happening to me there. I sat down on an empty stone bed in the room we found. Anon and Amira were incredibly tense around Zayika. I was intrigued to uncover more information about why I was included in their conflict and taken away from the life I once knew. Eager to learn more, I tried to keep my feelings in check. Zayika stated that the 'planet' would open up my mind to overwhelming opportunity while looming over me, her hair falling down by my side. Her green eyes were piercing and words flowed smoothly from her mouth with an air of confidence.

"So, Jameson. Let me tell you my story. Don't worry, I'll keep it short. I was placed into the Over Grounds faction. I play with stars. I can inflict injury with them in nearly any way that I choose." She looked at Anon briefly. "I can also heal others with them... and myself. Do you know what that means?"

"What are you trying to say?" I already made quiet assumptions about the type of person she was, but I wanted to ask questions and act more confused in order to get her to reveal as much as possible.

"I'm unstoppable. My destiny is to destroy those two right over there who are giving us dumbfounded expressions. This is because of their own doing, by the way, not mine. They are two-faced and use words that are full of deception. You should tune them out entirely." Her fingertips danced in the air on each syllable as she pointed over to Amira and Anon. "If there was an award for the worst couple to exist then they would get first place, no doubt about that. They're a match made in hell."

"Watch your words." Amira warned.

How come Zayika is so wrapped up in confrontation and destruction? I want to know more about her side in this. I knew what it was like to come into contact with others and walk away half-broken while they remain unscathed. *There are two sides to every story.*

"Why do you feel this way?" I asked Zayika as hatefulness radiated from her.

"Great question! The answer to that is what brought us all here, actually. There's been a bit of a... what would you guys call it?" She turned to the others while snapping her fingers. "Oh come on, can one of you help me out for once?"

"Butterfly effect." Amira finished her sentence with empty eyes.

"Exactly! Anon's many awful decisions have poisoned the roots of this planet and now they have grown! It's time to harvest the corrupted crops that he decided to plant in cursed soil." Zayika giggled and tapped her fingertips on her knees. "The full storm will be here soon."

"The blue trance." Anon said quietly.

"Now you're getting up to speed Jameson. Anon and his girlfriend decided to leave me behind to rot when they went back to Earth, even though they could have saved me too."

They didn't respond, but instead looked at each other to avoid her gaze.

"Really? You're too pretty to waste your life withering away on this planet." I told her.

"There's more to me than my outward appearance."

"I also sense that." *I want to know more.* "So you were entirely wronged?"

"Yes and I even saved his life before that. Two times. Don't associate yourself with them. They will screw you over, I promise."

"You know what's funny, Zayika? The fact that—" Anon started to walk over to us, but she sent a shockwave of gunmetal grey stars that went through his chest like bullets from a shotgun. He was flung backwards and hit the wall in anguish. The sound of his spine cracking filled the room. "What was that for? You can't let anyone else get a word in besides yourself?"

Blood oozed from his chest as she bit her finger playfully. "I'm just messing with you! That's a sneak peek of what's to come. I won't let you off that easily." At the speed of light, she sent stars his way again. This time they were sparkling yellow ones that began to heal him. "I can't let you die on me yet."

"Don't you ever do that again!" Amira was outraged.

"Get over it." Zayika snapped back. "He deserves some discomfort, and so will you if you don't get off my case."

"I'm not sure that I want to be a part of this." I proclaimed, about to get off of the stone.

"Trust me, Jameson, you should want an ability. Let me help change you. There was a man named Omar—"

"Keep his name out of your mouth." Anon interjected.

She ignored him and continued, "That had no abilities at all. He was very weak physically and mentally. He never got morphed and was of no use to this planet. Omar was the only one out of thirty who was not special in any way shape or form. Out here it's survival of the mentally fittest and if you fail... the planet will take you before anyone else can."

"What happened to him?" I asked.

"Omar's head was cracked open." Zayika made a cruel hand gesture and chuckled. "But I doubt that will happen to you. I can already tell that you are intended for a greater purpose than that poor bastard's unfortunate demise."

"I said keep his name out of your mouth!" Anon was about to shoot a lightning bolt towards Zayika and me with stiff arms. "Omar was my friend. He cared about me. You knew nothing about him! He shouldn't have died! You should have been the one tha—" He paused.

"I should have what? Been the one that died?" Zayika stood up and walked over to Anon. She put a hand on his shoulder with a surprised look. "But you can't even say that to me? You're that much of a coward? No wonder you got along with Omar... but interestingly enough you didn't even use your wish to revive him! Wow. Amira and Jameson, look at our caring hero. The one too busy trying to take a girl home that he valued literally no one else." Her words were dripping in disgust as she grabbed Anon by the throat and held him above her. "Don't tell me who I can or cannot talk about. You have no power over me and soon that will be clearer than ever before."

"Please put me down!" Anon tried clawing at her arm, but all of the deep scratches he left disappeared within seconds as she healed herself.

"You're a joke with no punchline." she snickered. "How humiliating."

I wasn't sure how to react for a few moments. *Is she going to hurt him?* I didn't want to interfere with the issues they had and was unsure exactly of whose words to trust, but Zayika was making one great point after the other. *Revenge can be a form of self-defense.*

Amira jumped in desperately. "Zayika, if you want to get back to Earth so badly, why didn't you just wait for someone new to get here who was also a Wish Carrier and play by the rules?"

I think I am a 'Wish Carrier'. Will I be hunted? Who exactly will be after me?

"You know what Amira? Waiting for a new round of fighting to start is a great idea. You are a genius." Zayika dropped Anon and shifted her gaze to the other woman. "It was actually in my head for a little while, but eventually got replaced as I wandered day after day and couldn't forget how you both betrayed me. I started to care less about going to Earth and instead more about you two coming to Eunoia. You should understand that there is satisfaction in revenge and closure. Didn't you work as a crime scene investigator? Try to tell me that there wasn't at least one case you studied where you rooted for someone to be put into their place. Eventually a perpetual victim will snap and fight back, and you can disagree with me on this, but when they do I don't think they are the one to blame. It's a shame that your career was to solve mysteries, but in your personal life you can't uncover the most obvious answers as to why you're backed into a corner."

Amira was left without a word to say as Anon punched the wall behind him in frustration.

"I don't understand what part I have in this." All three of them placed their attention on me again as I spoke up.

"Your purpose will be revealed after this, I promise." Zayika pointed towards the stone I was on which directed my attention to the fact that it had started glowing.

Something changed in me from within. The blood in my veins felt as though it was expanding like a balloon filled with water and about to pop. When I tried to pull myself upwards, a current held me down that pushed against me so hard that I thought my skin would tear from the pressure. I looked down as moss grew all over my body, which began to cover up every hair follicle as I resisted the urge to scratch at it. *What's going on?* I felt it creeping along my neck all the way down to my toes. There was a prickling sting in my pores, like every hair was being slowly plucked out by their roots with a pair of heated tweezers. I was flinching and trying to not holler as Zayika bent down and whispered into my ear, "I can make the pain go away."

One Week Before

Jameson clocked in for another weekly night shift at his town's convenience store. He picked up the job as a second way to bring in income for himself at twenty-six years old, looking for work after college. Very few people visited during the freezing winter nights. He periodically watched the clock's hands move while making sure to complete all of his assigned duties in a timely manner. Each aisle he walked down to take inventory of was clean with no customers in sight. The sound of his footsteps and music playing from his phone were the only things making noise as his shift slowly came to a close. He stood behind the counter and leaned over it with a palm resting on his chin. The tall glass windows showed a few cars passing by every once in a while, and he wondered if anyone would stop by before he was supposed to lock up. Large mounds of snow piled in the parking lot and speckles of it flew around amongst the burnt orange glow from nearby street lights.

After double checking the closing totals of cash and change in the register, Jameson turned its key sharply once, confirming that everything was there. He sat down into the chair behind him and began to slip into a deep sleep he couldn't resist. More time passed as another layer of snow gathered. It wasn't until a set of screeching brakes from outside jostled him awake with a racing heart. His eyes grew large as he stood up and went closer to the shop's entrance to get a better view of who was in such a hurry. He grinned as his friend exited the driver's seat and headed to the front door, but it quickly fell once he noticed a pistol gripped tightly in his left hand.

Present

"What do you mean?" I saw Zayika's reassuring smile beside me.

"You'll be fine. We've all been through this." she responded. "I think you're tough enough to survive — especially with me helping you."

She placed her warm fingertips on my quivering collarbones. Small yellow stars fell over my body as it was being changed. The pain was gone.

"What if he doesn't make it? Zayika, you know that some people can't survive the morphing process!" Anon shouted hastily.

She's taking away the pain, but what if I really don't survive this?

"Shut up Anon!" Zayika snapped while rolling her eyes. "You're going to make everything worse."

He was.

"He might have to go through this. No one currently has any wishes here to use." Amira responded to him, trying to be quiet, but I heard what she said next. "Anon, what if a Wish Carrier can't utilize their wish unless they've been morphed? That's something we're unsure of. I'm almost positive that he is a Carrier because of his dream."

Anon was irritated. "I guess you're right."

The process was finally over and ended much quicker than I expected. While panting, I touched my arms and legs trying to make sense of what sprang out of me. I looked infected. There was a moldy looking substance in between the moss and green strings that fell off my body.

"Looks like you're wearing a camouflage suit." Zayika kindly ran both sets of her fingers over my shoulders. "You look good. Could come in handy for stealth."

"Zayika, are you kidding me?" Anon charged over to us. "Is this what you brought Amira and me back for? To watch you begin recruiting your own personal army on Eunoia?"

"That's a great idea, Anon, that sounds really badass." She nodded her head enthusiastically. "But no, I have to finish you off, thanks for reminding me. This has been fun Jameson. I'm going to urge you to go find out what ability you were given. Why not join the fight we're about to get into? I promise I'll let you have a few good hits at Anon and I'll heal you if anything goes sideways."

I didn't have several options. "Um…" I sat up. "I guess I'll join."

"This is crazy!" Anon exasperatedly put both hands on the top of his head. "Fine. Let's do this. I'm tired of time being wasted."

"That's a cute comment coming from the man who left me on this planet for days on end. I think I can steal a bit of your time, seeing as though you've taken a good amount of mine."

Anon's arms lit up. "Get over it! Oh my goodness, just get over it! You were here alone with the representatives for what, a few weeks? You were so impatient to wait for others that you needed to miserably drag us down with you?"

Zayika leapt forwards and stood tall in front of him to look down at his face. "I wouldn't have had to wait for others at all if you used your wish on me."

"Amira didn't either!" Anon kept yelling.

"You're really going to try to throw her under the bus? She wasn't from the same faction as us, so you not helping me was worse." Zayika looked at Amira and grinned. "But I still think that you are horrible too."

Anon's voice sounded broken, like he was on the verge of giving up his attempts to put up a fight. "You of all people should understand me. You should understand why we used our wishes the way that we did."

"Why is that? Please tell me. I'm on the edge of my seat practically dying to kno—"

"Because Zayika. We chose our wishes selfishly." He backed away to exit through the door.

Amira cleared her throat.

"No!" Zayika screamed. "You're not calling me selfish and then walking away like a complete coward!" She launched stars at him from her palms that wrapped over his waist and yanked him to the floor. "Fight me! Come on, fight me! Fight me like you fought Nathaniel! If you are going to act brave then prove that you are, Anon!"

"Zayika, this is ridiculous!" he groaned while trying to get up. "Why can't you see that?"

"Don't tell me you're scared you will lose right now in front of Amira." Zayika bent over and murmured into Anon's ear close to where I was standing. "I'll give you some unsolicited advice. If you want to impress her, which you clearly do, you might not want to walk out of the room throwing a temper tantrum. I think Amira might be more excited about a guy who can actually face his issues."

Anon swung and grabbed onto Zayika's face. He launched a ray of lightning through her eyes and open mouth as she wailed out in pain. "Hold your tongue." he told her in a lowered voice.

"Get your filthy hand off of me!" she demanded.

"We need to end this!" Amira placed her hand on Anon's lower back.

Zayika took her leg and kicked his stomach with as much force as she could muster. "You're right. We need to end this!" She put her hands on either side of her head that was clearly throbbing. "Let's make this a fair fight. We are going outside. Amira, let's see what you're capable of without your slimy fish doing all of the work for you. And Jameson... let's see what you can do too."

"Are you ready to die, Zayika?" Anon asked while glaring at her through strands of his jet black hair.

"Sounds like the question you need to be asking yourself." she responded.

I gulped as a bout of excitement fluttered in my chest and followed the three outside to a large courtyard. There were overgrown plants everywhere, cracked pebble stones to walk on, and thick roots coming out of them from gigantic swaying trees. *I will defend myself if I have to. I can't forget to look out for myself.* For some reason the other's eyes were looking at every single stone as Anon's expression showed a glimpse of what I could only guess was regret. *If Anon didn't kill that woman in the jungle... then who did? Are they still here?*

"So where's Nathaniel's body?" Zayika skipped around in her thigh-high boots.

"Doesn't matter." Anon replied. "By the way, what happened to your hair? I've been meaning to bring that up. It looks different."

"It was half silver before right?" Amira joined in.

"Ha! Stop pretending like you guys don't remember. You're terrible at acting." She laughed. "Something within me changed my hair."

"By 'something' you mean passive aggressive behavior and psychopathic tendencies, right?" Anon responded.

"You're becoming wittier." Zayika stepped over to Anon. "I like that. It's a shame that the likable side of your personality didn't start developing until now."

I awkwardly stood near an oversized tree, leaning my back against it and tapping my foot on its bark. "I'm not sure why I'm here."

Zayika pointed a finger at me. "Thank you for redirecting us again, wow, we are getting so off track, aren't we? Sorry. I don't want to waste your time." She put both her palms out at me and I stared at her. "You didn't flinch? Shocking. Maybe I'm just so used to everyone else being petrified if I so much as look at them. Impressive Jameson. You are a bit... impressive."

It was hard to not smirk. "Thanks, you are too."

"But we need to really find out just how impressive you are." Zayika threw her long purple hair behind her shoulders and spoke to Anon and Amira, "Let's allow the newcomer to try out what he was given in the morphing process before we get to finishing our business. It's only fair."

Amira and Anon shrugged in unison. I could see the underlying fear in their eyes even though they were trying to put up a front for Zayika. *She really gets under their skin, doesn't she? Creating tension is a pastime for her.*

The attention was on me again. "What do you want me to do?" I asked.

Zayika got up very close to my face. "Do you mind if I help?"

All I want is a better understanding. "Go ahead."

She placed her hands on my forearms and let out a deep breath. "Relax. Close your eyes. Start breathing in and don't take a break until you begin to sense your power. You might feel like you'll pass out… but you won't. You'll be okay."

I followed her instructions, unsure of what else to do. I wanted to be able to defend myself and wasn't scared to fight. I wasn't a complete stranger to dealing with the unpredictability of others. *Trust their words. I need to believe that I'm a Carrier and get home so I can make my life right. There is no choice but to play along.* When I only paid attention to what I could tangibly feel, it was as if I was the only person present at that moment. I kept my eyelids shut and felt air entering and exiting my lungs. A source of energy from Zayika brought me to a heightened sense of enlightenment and inner strength. The ground beneath my feet started to vibrate. I opened my eyes as dirt lifted and uncovered a surprisingly large weapon. *Is that a grenade launcher?* I was yearning to try out the new weapon by my side and pick who to assist with it.

"Wow." Zayika knelt down beside it. "That will come in handy. Right Anon and Amira? Are you both ready to dodge some explosions?"

I picked it up and a faint white outline appeared over its edges. I aimed it into the air and adjusted to how holding it felt. Once I located its firing pin, I attempted to let a round out of it that was directed away from the others. The launcher released a fiery explosion that caused part of the jungle to instantaneously light up into flames as everything grew scolding hot around us. Zayika shrugged at the fire spreading as if it was not a big deal and the other two observed me worriedly.

"Be careful!" Anon said rigidly.

"Give it another shot, Jameson!" Zayika encouraged me to try again.

There seems to be no reloading required… or safety included. My feelings changed to excitement instead of curiosity when I prepared to shoot it again. I felt ready to face any threat that the planet was going to throw my way. *Why was this weapon given to me?* The next grenade was different from the previous one. It exploded in a similar way but gave off a blue ray of smoke as it hit the ground and started to freeze over the vines and bushes that it came into contact with.

"How are you changing what type of ammo it's using?" Anon moved out of the way from where I was firing.

"That's pretty cool, actually." Amira interjected.

"Come on!" Anon motioned at her to follow him. "Don't get close to this stuff!"

Zayika laughed near my side. "Stop worrying so much, Anon, I promise that I won't let one of these grenades kill you."

"Should I try once more?" *Why am I smiling?* I was ready to attack something and discover what other types of ammunition that the launcher could spawn. *Hopefully I don't run out of shots when I need them.*

"Definitely, do it again." Zayika got nearer to me and watched my weapon closely. "I've never seen a Land Dweller operate like this before."

I nodded my head and pointed it up to the turbulent sky again and got my pointer finger ready. This time, for some reason, I decided to aim closer to where Amira and Anon were standing. *Let's just see what happens.*

"Wait!" Anon noticed how I was focused in their direction. "What are you doi—"

Click. The grenade released and flew towards them. In only a few seconds, there was a loud booming sound that came from it as a huge gust of smoke covered them entirely.

"That was a smoke grenade!" he yelled.

"Thanks for stating the obvious." Zayika retorted. "Do it one more time, Jameson, it's time for you to hit living beings instead of shrubbery."

Something from within prompted me to follow her instructions without asking questions. Zayika's words made me want to impress her. But before I could see what grenade was to follow, the other two used the smoke to get away from us. We only saw a small glimpse of Anon using his wings while holding Amira to fly as far away as they could get.

What came over me? How am I going to use this energy and power? Who am I against?

Zayika put a fist up at them and then spoke to me. Her voice pierced through my invisible wall of self-defense and opened it up into growing eagerness.

"Jameson. I can tell that you're on the fence right now. You are not sure what side to help, or if you want to help any of us out at all, and that's okay. If you do not want to fight alongside me or even believe my story then I won't judge you. I know that what I say sounds crazy... but believe me that it's all true."

I remained quiet. She was showing a side of herself that I wasn't sure others had seen before.

"I need you to know that Amira and Anon do not care about you even if they act like they do. Watch your back. I wouldn't be surprised if they try to sneak out from the sidelines and kill you to get your wish if you end up being a Carrier."

"I believe I am one based on what's been said and done, but I don't think they'll do that."

"You're that trusting of them already?" she asked.

"No. I say that because if they did that to me and went back to Earth the same way you said before... who's to say you wouldn't just bring them here once more and repeat all of this again?"

She smiled. "You'd be surprised at how many people here repeat the history of their past mistakes and never learn from them. They are the kinds who don't care for others that they deem as unnecessary. They're so blinded by their own interests that they don't stop to think about the interests of others, even those who have sacrificed for them. It would be a stupid choice for them to repeat the past, but unfortunately I wouldn't expect them to be smarter than that. I can't give them too much credit."

I felt my lips curve downwards as I shared another thought with her, "But Zayika... you know that if they kill me and get another wish then they could not only ask to go home but... ask for you to die?"

I'm sure that's the only way they can defeat her.

It was clear by her thunderstruck expression that she hadn't thought about that loophole. For the first time since meeting her I was actually seeing Zayika speechless. We both stood in silence at my words as Anon and Amira were presumably arriving at the ocean's shore. She had both hands on her hips and knocked her boot against the weeds growing out of the ground. I observed her as she stayed silent. Her eyes and body language seemed desperate for relief. *What is she thinking?* It was clear how much of a mental toll the others' actions were taking on her. I felt like asking more questions but had no idea where to start. *Is she the one in the right here? Is all of this a case of betrayal and revenge? I want to help her, but I need to be sure that doing so is the right call.*

"Thank you for bringing that to my attention." She tried to save face. "Make sure they don't kill you, okay? I'm pretty sure you were already planning on not letting that happen. I'm going after them. If you join my side in this, I will keep you healed in battle. I won't let you die. If you go your own way, then your outcome completely falls on you. Remember, Jameson, that you have potential. With your wish you are worth more than you realize. I don't have a problem with you unless you try to help them with it. I have to go."

I watched as she ran away, using maroon-colored stars to move even faster with them fluttering all around her. *What should I do? I could help her, but that means killing the other two. Anon and Amira seemed trustworthy earlier. I don't think they would harm me. But who knows? If I don't join either side, then I'm left to completely fend for myself. What should I do?*

I started walking towards a different path in the jungle to figure out what steps to take next. The weather brought on increased feelings of dreariness and dread as the night was coming to a close. I decided to look around for something to eat or drink since the tree house had been wiped clean. Morning was bound to bring along a new host of intense issues. Minutes were passing by rapidly as I was desperate to be shown or told the right way to go. I was getting lost amongst vines and rocky pathways. I needed to decide who I would support and use my wish for. *I have to pick whose side to be on… but what do I choose when they are apparently both on mine?* Upon my final thought, there was a loud noise nearby which sounded like a vacuum being turned on. There was a man's voice that seemed to bounce off of the leaves near me and I heard him say... "Saige?"

CHAPTER SIX: TRANQUIL ABYSS

Zekiel

Present

Being transported into the unknown was a difficult experience to put into words. Nero forced me through a portal with him after I removed his second wing. At that time, I felt nothing but contempt for him. He murdered Saige, the truest friend I had, and my mind was running rampant. He yanked me by my hair into oblivion, leaving me unable to fight back. My vision was lost for a few minutes while the sounds of rushing air grew so loud that I was on the verge of deafness. The feeling of loss swallowed me whole like a ravenous monster. It felt as though I was losing my freedom as the jungle before me gradually vanished.

Saige's bloody face was the last thing I saw before we both completely disappeared. *Why did she have to sacrifice herself?* With each second it felt more and more like I didn't deserve her admiration and commitment. Right before everything fell apart, she admitted to being romantically interested in me. *Why?* I told her that it wasn't mutual… which took me a while to do. I could hardly focus on my own self let alone be present for the thoughts and feelings of another person. I always knew it would've been irresponsible for me to let her down, but I ended up doing exactly that. *There must've been so many subtle signs of flirtation that I missed.* It was nearly impossible to comprehend what was going on in her head since mine was a tangled mess of its own.

When entering the portal I recalled various memories with my girlfriend Jasmine and her lovely presence. Then I thought about Saige and what she did for me. *I don't want to hurt any longer. I can't go on with my own life while they do not have theirs anymore.* The two were selfishly taken from the world at the hands of others who had nothing good to offer. Nero and the driver who killed my girlfriend deserved to pay for the crimes they committed. My chest was tight and my eyes were dry until all of a sudden... they weren't anymore. It was as if the void cured me once I was finally completely inside of it. Beautiful stars flowed around me and I could no longer think about what shredded up my mind entirely. *Is this what peacefulness is?*

Then I fell into a deep sleep for a long time until an intruder woke me. I went from floating within pure everlasting silence in one moment to being back on a treacherous planet in the next. I took several stumbles trying to walk at first and fell onto my aching knees. *How much time has passed?* With unsteady hands, I grabbed at dirty vines below me. My skin changed from its normal state back to what it was like when I was morphed. Bark painfully grew out of it again and cavities in my chest were reforming. *How unfortunate. This can't be happening...* I looked behind me, hoping to see the portal open for the void again, wishing to see the tunnel that swept Nero and me away, but it wasn't there. *No, no, no!* It was gone without a trace just like everyone in my life that I cared for. To my misfortune I was taken to the Land Dweller terrain in the exact place that I was stripped from. *That means…*

With bated breath I turned to see her. "Saige?" I spoke aloud while falling onto the rocky dirt below and crawled to where her body was laying. "Saige, no." I took her into my arms.

There was rotting flesh on some of her bones and the blade which split her face open was rusted with bugs crawling over it. I yanked it out and threw it as far as I could. I did nothing but sob for a while. While rocking back and forth, my mind was tortured by the memory of what she did. *She shouldn't have stepped in front of me! Why did she take the blade?* But I knew the answer to my own question. Saige was selfless in her love for me. I didn't want to wallow in sorrow but allowed myself to exist in it for as long as I could mentally bear. Eventually, it was time to move on—painfully similar to the aftermath of losing Jasmine.

A plan arose within me to get back to the void and not return to being trapped on Earth or Eunoia's mental playground. *I can't leave Saige out here like this.* I stood up and started scouring around to find the right materials to dig a hole and give her a proper burial. There was a cluster of plants from the jungle that I tied together with a vine to lay over Saige's burial site. I spoke the only words I could manage with what I'm sure looked like a sunken expression, "Saige. You were always there. No matter the circumstances, your unconditional thoughtfulness always remained present. Thank you for your care and for being able to love someone who is broken like me." Tears fell. "I loved our friendship and I promise that I will never, ever forget it. I won't ever forget you."

Five Years Before

Zekiel held tightly onto the handle of his umbrella while watching Jasmine's casket being lowered into the ground. A tragic car accident stole the life of his girlfriend and he struggled greatly with processing everything that happened. He was unable to cry after doing so constantly since receiving the phone call informing him of her death. Both parents were by his left side grabbing tissues from their pockets and Saige was at his right. She wiped away a few tears that escaped and shakily tucked a handful of straight hair behind her ear. Zekiel inhaled sharply and watched the clouds; he couldn't bring himself to look at anyone nearby. A part of him wanted to attend the funeral alone to mourn in utter silence and physical distance away from everyone he knew.

"I'm so sorry this happened, Zeek." Saige spoke slowly. "If there's anything I can do please let me know. I'm not sure what to say."

"I prefer silence." he responded.

"Of course."

He was thankful that she understood what he needed, which was to not discuss the heartache at all. Eventually the others left, one by one, from the grassy field and back to their cars to head home. Zekiel and Saige stood still and didn't leave until they were the last two paying their respects to Jasmine. He took the bouquet of purple and white flowers he picked out earlier and gracefully laid them down in front of her gravestone.

"I love you Jasmine. Rest in peace."

Present

Tears kept falling as I ventured onwards and left Saige behind me. I went to wipe off my face, but instead scratched my skin with the rough bark along my palm and wrist. I didn't allow myself to think for a while. No thoughts... they were unbearable. I needed silence in my mind.

Only silence. Just like how the void's atmosphere was — empty beyond comprehension. *Where are the representatives?* Although my mind was flooding with grief, it also became infected with questions. *Who else is here? What happened while I was away?* I found myself walking faster until I eventually went into a complete sprint. *Is there no one else around?* I couldn't believe my eyes. There was no other person in sight for what seemed to be a very long time. Silhouettes of tree branches tricked me in my peripheral vision while running through the crisp early morning. *Who won the wishes to escape?*

I began calling out, "Hello? Is anyone there?"

The empty planet made it feel as though I was in the void again, but alone in the most unpleasant way. No one was in or around the Land Dweller building. *There are no signs of life.* After leaving the area I was the most familiar with, I headed towards undiscovered places beyond my faction's grounds. My vision got blurry from the stress and so I paid an inadequate amount of attention to where I was going. I fumbled with my footing again and almost fell down into a trench next to a large murky and hazardous looking pond. *Have I reached the edge of the planet?*

"You might want to be careful." an unfamiliar voice told me.

A person?

"Who is out there?"

"My name is Jameson. I heard you yelling earlier, are you doing okay? Were you recently brought here too?"

Someone new? How long was I in the void?

"No. I-I've been here for quite some time." I responded hesitantly. *Don't tell him too much.*

"By your tree-like appearance I'm going to go out on a limb to make the assumption that you were also changed on a stone bed?"

His words prompted me to look closer. *Can he disappear like Saige could?* When I located him, I realized that he was blending in very well with the jungle as if he was wearing a high quality camouflage suit.

"You've spotted me." He walked towards where I stood, carefully treading along the outline of the pond down by his feet. "You said you've been here for a while. Does that mean you could help me out? Something supernatural happened to me in that building." He pointed to my faction. "My body has been destroyed."

I gave him a guarded look and prompt handshake. "It's nice to meet you, though I'm sorry you've been brought here. I am Zekiel."

"I'm working on getting home."

"Are you a Wish Carrier?" *I'm sure he doesn't know what I'm talking about. Why even ask?*

"I think so."

He seems trusting of others… very quickly.

I let go of his hand quickly and stepped backwards. "How do you know what I'm talking about? Did you read the planet's stone?"

"No. I've never even seen it. There was a dream that led me here, a painful one, and the others that I met told me about what this place is and how I'm apparently different."

"Who are 'the others' you're referring to?"

"Their names are..." he paused. "Amira, Zayika, and Anon."

How are they still here? Wouldn't they have gotten back to Earth?

"Really?" I was in disbelief.

"Yes. You know who I'm talking about?"

"Definitely. Where did you last see them?"

"At the giant treehouse. They're at war with each other. Zayika's really trying to do a number on both and, if I'm being honest, I don't want to get caught in the middle of their problems."

"I don't blame you. I think we might get along well." I pushed some hair away from my eyes to see the new face in front of me clearer. "Take me to where they are and on the way we can discuss what to do next."

"Sounds like a plan." Jameson responded while leading me in the direction he came from.

The pond next to us suddenly started bubbling as we were walking. I picked up a rock and skipped it along the top of the stewing liquid. Several colorful plants were growing in front of it that looked full of poisonous darts and the other side near us was surrounded with overgrown trees and bushes which made our pathway more constricted.

"Watch your step." Jameson stated. "Earlier I heard some odd sounds over here before we met."

I nodded in response and we continued onwards. I wasn't in the mood to talk. A lot of time passed since I'd interacted with another being. *Be personable... at least try.* "What is your life like at home?" I forced myself to ask.

"No worries, dude, we don't have to talk about that kind of stuff." he responded.

"Oh. Great." I laughed out loud briefly—something I hadn't done in a very long time, which was like a shot of medicine sent straight into my soul.

"Yeah, I know. I've heard enough of it from the other three and my story really isn't a great conversation starter to be frank."

"Neither is mine."

"Sounds like we know where we stand."

"The sky looks a bit terrifying, doesn't it?" I asked him. It was much different compared to how I saw it before vanishing. A distinct purple mixed with a rich pink hue was creeping around, slowly dominating the greenish blue that was once there. It felt like the planet was closing in around us as we went onwards and rain kept starting and stopping. *Saige was not given the life she deserved. She tried to look after me, but everything went wrong so viciously.* Wind whistled past my ears as I kept my thoughts to myself. *Why were we brought here? How did the planet know about our friendship? Why did it make sure she woke up beside me? Will I ever get to see Jasmine again and tell her I love her once more?* My head was aching. *Will I get to thank Saige for her selflessness?*

"I can tell that a storm is near." Jameson glanced upwards.

"We'll want to get closer to cover."

There was a sound coming from the pond not far from where we were. We looked at each other and back at it for a few moments, unsure of what could be making the noise. *It could be an earthquake forming, but then why aren't other parts of the planet shaking?* Rays of colorful smoke arose as something enormous pushed its way towards us. There was a rugged and pointy pattern emerging from the water as a creature revealed more of itself. *Is that a reptile?*

A monstrous crocodile appeared before us as we both held our breaths. *We can't startle it... be careful.* It was unlike anything I'd ever seen before with massive eyes that glowed like purple stoplights. There were several rows of teeth the size of surfboards that filled the entirety of its mouth and scars covering every inch of its face. I tapped my fingertips nervously against each other while trying to stay incredibly still.

"Jameson." I said in a hushed tone. "Don't make any sudden movements."

"I won't." he responded reassuringly.

There's absolutely no way we could pry those jaws off of us if it gets a chance to bite down. We'll be crushed in seconds.

Jameson stood bravely with what looked to be a grenade launcher in his hands. I glanced down at my arms, certain that we could at least stun the creature momentarily to get away. *Be careful using this ability.* The bark growing on my skin made using fire bursts very harmful for me if I didn't pay attention to how severe the flames were.

"What does your weapon do?" I whispered. "Have you tested it?"

The crocodile's head turned slowly, which created a gust of wind over us as it moved. We both were putting our arms up to shield our vision from its beaming iridescent eyes. One of them fixated intently on us from the side. It began opening up its massive jaw further and slightly lunged closer. *It's ready to snap.*

"Thankfully, yes." he looked at me heroically. "I can launch a variety of grenades. Cyro, fire, smoke... you name it and I'll probably have it. The category seems to depend on how I'm feeling."

It was refreshing to work with someone who could assist me in taking on the newfound threat. *He adapts quickly… but I have to strategize.* It was already evident that Jameson wasn't unobservant; he knew that letting down our guard would result in being torn open before we could even blink.

"Alright. I'll throw a flame round at him. Can you do some type of damage alongside that?"

His teeth glistened with a candid smile. "Let's get this kill under our belt."

I took his words as a cue to warm up my palms. I rubbed them together hastily and blew a breath of air into them. *It's been a while, but I can do this.* I took a few slow steps toward the crocodile as it remained perfectly still. One of its vibrant eyes centered directly on me. *Stay still… do not attack… we can't die like this.* I sent a bolt of fire forwards and Jameson stepped in with an explosive blast shortly thereafter. The enemy hissed with such great force that the planet shook beneath our feet once more. It gyrated its body to redirect itself closer, charging up a relentless bite with a menacing dive.

"Don't hurt Ghoul!" The unfamiliar voice was like a shock wave over the murky pond. "Leave him alone!"

"Who is speaking?" I didn't let my guard down.

A young man climbed down from one of the trees, using the vines to safely guide him while peering over a jittering shoulder. We got a better look at him once he finally reached the ground. His skin was pale and had long black hair that blended in with his ripped clothing. The crocodile gave an intimidating snarl, which caused Jameson to spring into action.

"Watch out!" he said to the stranger.

The person we met wasn't scared by the mutant but instead filled with fear at us as we observed him.

"Why would I?" he said in an unsure tone. "He's not going to hurt me."

This must be a companion assigned to him for a fighting ability. He has also been called to be a Land Dweller.

"Don't sic it on us. I have reason to believe that we are of the same faction." I told him. "I'm Zekiel and this is Jameson, who was also brought here recently. What is your name?"

None of us reached out to shake hands. *Refrain from being hostile.*

"I'm Yestin. There have been sounds of laughter and shouts in the distance, but I haven't seen who they belong to yet. You're the first people I've met face to face. I've been staying out of sight."

"Really?" I refrained from scoffing. "That's odd. You haven't seen a woman running about with neon hair or a man with lightning in his arms?"

Yestin laughed at my genuine concerns. "No, definitely not, I think I would remember them if I did."

"How long have you been on this planet?" Jameson asked.

"I'm… not sure. I found my way to this jungle after appearing on a group of widespread hills. I tried to rest on a bed of stone not too far from here, but it was a bad idea. I've felt sick ever since entering that building. This monster came to me and has stayed by my side since."

"Let me guess… you had a strange encounter with someone at a certain place?" I predicted what he was going to share.

"Yeah. You did too?" Yestin tapped his foot on the ground nervously. "My brother Varid went missing at our town's waterfall. Our family has been so broken since his disappearance. I went out myself trying to look for him and ended up being abducted and taken here. There were clouds covering the entire sky on the night he was gone. Now I feel like I'm living in the storm that was there when he went away. I've been jinxed too."

"Interesting." *What should I say?* "Well, Yestin, there's a lot that I can try to explain to you."

"Like what?" His silver eyes showed intrigue.

Why did someone else have to appear? I don't have the energy for this. Everything is so complicated in my own mind, let alone having to carry along two new fighters with me. I want peace and quiet. How do I speed this along? I engulfed my palms with fire in the midst of frustrated thoughts, which I didn't realize at first, but their facial expressions told me otherwise.

"What are you doing?" Jameson stepped backwards.

"Are you an enemy?" Yestin put a hand on the creature's spiky side beside him and squinted.

"N-no. I'm not the 'enemy'." *Get it together. Just speak. Use my words and diffuse this situation.*

I couldn't get the flames to subside. A round flew out and struck a nearby bush, which burned to a crisp. Another escaped shortly after.

"Man! Get your head on right!" Jameson lifted his gun, which I thought he aimed at me, but it was at the crocodile fixating on us again.

"You're freaking him out!" Yestin tried to tell me.

Cool down! The fire seeping from my hands started to eat away at the bark growing where my skin used to be. The pain was indescribable. *Cool down, now!*

"It's releasing something!" Jameson called out and ducked.

A row of its razor-sharp teeth flew in our direction. Ghoul made a rumbling growl as the next layer of teeth began rotating forwards, revealing its endless supply to use against us. I bolted past one that was coming straight for me and braced myself near the ground by another that already fell. *What is on this?* I quickly got a closer look at the crocodile's fang and noticed what seemed to be human flesh and intestines sticking to it.

The monster lunged at me with determination. Jameson thought quickly and shot off a grenade attack aimed near its back. I tried to leap forwards, completely out of harm's way, and while doing so one of the crocodile's front teeth cut deeply into my right thigh. I tried to control my reaction and not wear my emotions on my sleeve. Jameson asked if I was alright and I couldn't bring myself to answer him at that moment. *Keep moving! Get out of this!* My internal thoughts were unbearable screams, but I kept a straight face despite the circumstance.

Yestin yelled again, "You're making Ghoul angry! Stop!"

Out of the corner of my eye I could see it heading straight for Jameson with a hungry gaze. *Save him and then your own self later!* Without a second thought I sent off a wave of fire past Jameson's right side, but my aim was off, and I accidentally hit Yestin instead. He screamed in agony while being burned alive. The foul smell of burning flesh filled the air and at first I was unsure if it was his, mine, or both. Everything seemed out of focus. Blurry vision was ailing me. I tried to pull myself into reality and witness the unfolding events from a clearer perspective. I watched as he rolled around on the ground and heard his ear-piercing voice pleading for us to save him.

"Why did you hit him?" Jameson leaned over where I was on the ground. "Hey! Zekiel! He's dying!"

I used my elbows and kneecaps to pull myself up along the dirt. *This leads to a path that could take us away from the pond. We have to go!* The crocodile was still after us with newfound vengeance for killing his companion. *We can't defeat it!* Enough blood was escaping rapidly through my jagged wound to make me lightheaded within moments. *I need to stop the bleeding!* Echoes of Yestin's screams were like a boomerang as I winced at the sound.

"Zekiel! Are you alright?" Jameson launched another shot at the groaning creature as he ran over to check on me again. "We need to get out of here! Are you going to be okay?"

I slowly closed my eyelids and responded, "I don't know."

CHAPTER SEVEN: RAINDROPS

Jameson

Present

Most of my energy was gone after fighting the massive crocodile that attacked Zekiel and me. He was wounded as I carried him along through the jungle far away from the treacherous pond. Hot beads of sweat fell down my face as I leaned onto my kneecaps and waited to see what he thought about the entire ordeal. He surprisingly seemed very collected, almost like he was completely unscathed and definitely not as though he had just killed someone. *Why is he acting this way?* Zekiel was almost maimed in the fight. A devastating chunk of flesh was missing from his right leg. He hardly showed any signs of affliction as he tore off a piece of his shirt and tied it tightly over the wound.

There was a lot I didn't know about him. *I should learn more. What if I could strategize with him? This guy tried to save my life... but can I trust someone who can't control their temper? He seems unpredictable.* My judgement was askew. *Who can I trust?* Zekiel killed the man we met named Yestin with his flames, but I could tell that it was unintentional. The situation we were in went from bad to worse in a matter of minutes when the stranger came down from the tree and tried to defend his pet crocodile. Even after leaving, I could still miserably smell Yestin burning alive and hear his screams echoing behind us.

It didn't seem like I was in any danger by traveling with Zekiel, but the only thing that concerned me about his behavior was how strictly reserved he was. I didn't expect others to make conversation all of the time or open up a lot about their lives, but something about him seemed as though it surpassed that level of wanting privacy. *There must be a lot going on in his mind.* He told me that he knew Zayika, Amira, and Anon. I was extremely interested in seeing them all reunite. *Who else is in this place besides us?*

Zekiel tore away at fabric from the jean jacket he was wearing to make a tourniquet. "Wait... this alone won't do it... I'm hardly thinking right now." he said to himself in a hushed tone.

"We're lucky to have made enough distance from that thing."

It was challenging to get him to speak after what happened. For a little while I followed behind him as he searched for something. Zekiel kept one of his hands pressed hard against the fabric where blood was escaping. There was almost a sign of relief from him when we stumbled upon a pile of scrap amongst broken crates and vines. He drew out flames from his palm and placed it onto the first metal rod he could find.

"Have to cauterize the wound." His expression changed only slightly at the burning flesh as he targeted the large area of himself that was damaged.

Is this guy serious? "That's a bit intense, man."

"Has to be done." he responded while trying to keep his cool.

"Zayika could have healed you. She can do that with stars." I told him.

"I wouldn't risk wasting time to find her with the amount of blood that has left my body." He started to continue on with our journey, seemingly unfazed by the crocodile and searing pain. "But thanks for letting me know that, though. Good for her."

"Yeah. She seems to have a lot going for her with that ability. Plus, she's gorgeous." I replied.

"Be a bit careful when it comes to her." Zekiel spoke quickly.

"Did you know her well in the past?"

"She was someone who I traveled with before we all got separated into different factions. I don't know her extremely well, but all I will say is that I don't think it's wise to get on her bad side."

"The same could be said for you, right? I mean... are we going to talk about what happened back there?"

"What?" Zekiel asked with resistance. "Do we have to? Because I'd rather not."

"Sorry. That was an awful joke." I cringed while continuing, "I'm not going to scold you for what happened if that's what you think. I know you were aiming for the mutant, not Yestin."

"It was extremely embarrassing." He shifted his attention to the ground again as we walked along. "My aim is awful."

"That's not really your fault, though, is it? I mean it doesn't seem like you've been fighting a lot here."

"There haven't been a lot of opportunities to. Not like I'm complaining, I'm tired of conflict and sick of lives being wasted." He whispered to himself, "Damn my awful aim and stunted arms."

"You seem more concerned with your aim than you are about Yestin. Is it because you didn't even know him?"

That came out wrong.

Zekiel stared at me. "Don't use my words against me, please. Of course I was distraught about killing that man accidentally, are you kidding? But if I let myself feel that regret... I'm not sure what I would do. Let me distract myself."

I placed my fingers along the weapon at my side while navigating what to say next. "Let's leave it behind us then. You tried to save me. That's what happened."

His tone gave off a hint of disbelief, "Really? You don't want to part ways?"

It's better to have him as an ally... not a foe. "Yeah. Let's just try to get back to Earth. That's the goal, right?"

"Sure."

Change the conversation to lighten the mood. Gain more knowledge from a broader perspective. "What else do you know about the other three? Zayika, Anon, and Amira?"

"Well Jameson... they are going to be an integral part in our journey back home."

"How exactly?"

"I've begun devising a plan that involves them. I was trapped in a time warp and now that I'm out of it I want to make sure I do my part to finally return to Earth. I belonged to the Land Dweller's faction as you can probably tell by my appearance and abilities. My chance to get a wish and go home wasn't meant to be back then."

"What's your plan?"

"Anon has both his wings, right?"

"Yeah."

"He's what's going to save us. When a man from the Over Ground's faction loses both of their wings, the portal opens—the one I was in. I will hack them off and you can use your ability to force Zayika into the void that appears."

Am I alright with getting rid of Zayika? I haven't even gotten to really know her yet... "How do we get home after that?"

"We find one of the representatives and use your wish to get taken back."

"That sounds like a good plan." *Forget about her right now. I have to focus on staying alive.*

Zekiel seemed a bit taken back by my adamant response. "You're okay with it? This is not freaking you out?"

"No." *He doesn't know what I've been through.*

He nodded with a stoic expression and kept to himself for the greater part of what felt like an hour as we continued on to complete the freshly made plan. I decided to refrain from saying anything else at that time because I didn't want Zekiel to become overwhelmed again. I made sure to tiptoe in conversations with him very lightly, careful to not awaken his ability again and have myself get caught in the literal crossfire of his concealed emotions. *Hopefully there is not another instance of him losing control of himself like that.* We began heading to the ocean, hopeful that we could make it work, but for some reason there was skepticism building inside of me. Our plan seemed too good to be true.

One Week Before

Jameson's friend, Merrick, bolted towards him with a raised weapon and desperation in his eyes. The air was tense as the two stared at each other. Flickering fluorescent lights glistened over them as they analyzed the other's expression. Jameson looked at the security cameras in each corner of the room and then back at the pistol being held by his friend.

"What are you doing?" he asked Merrick.

"Empty the register."

Jameson went back to being seated, trying to stay calm, and lowered his voice to continue asking questions, "Y-you were serious about this?"

"I was, and it seemed that you were also sure about not making this difficult."

"Yeah, but..."

"Hurry up." Merrick demanded as he checked over his shoulder.

Jameson unlocked the register and looked at the piles of cash inside of it.

"Damn it! Someone is coming inside!" Merrick's hand started quivering while he kept the loaded weapon aimed.

He was right. Another car pulled into the parking lot near his vehicle. It wasn't long until Jameson realized that one of his coworkers arrived for a late night shopping run and was heading towards them.

"Is everything okay?" She let the glass door close softly before her steps came to a halt.

"Everything is fine." Merrick replied to her without turning around. He kept his eyes fixated on Jameson. "Right?"

"Um." He shifted back and forth on his feet. "Don't worry about it, Calla."

Her curiosity piqued. "Who are you? Is that a gun in your hand? I-I can tell that you are hiding it. Jameson is everything ok—"

Merrick twisted around to face her and revealed her suspicions to be true. "This doesn't involve you."

"It doesn't involve him either! Leave him alone!" she pleaded. "I'm calling the cops!"

"Turn away, Merrick. We don't need any trouble here tonight." Jameson got off of the barstool supporting him. "I seriously thought you were joking about this." he said in a lowered voice to his friend.

"Really? You're an idiot." Merrick shot Calla in the chest without hesitation as she began to dial 911. "How can you be such a bad judge of character?" He then fired off another one at the security camera that was recording them.

The room started spinning. Jameson watched as Calla yelled out for help while clutching the wound. Merrick set his gun down on the countertop and decided to focus his energy on kicking her in the stomach.

"Stop your yelling! This is what you get for interfering where you aren't welcome!" he clamored while pulling a knife out of his front pocket. "Shoot her in the head or else I'll finish this personally. We'll get rid of her body tonight. Make sure you also grab that cash for me."

Jameson thought for only one second on what to do next. He took a hold of the pistol and swallowed the lump that grew in his throat. "I'm not a bad judge of character."

The trigger was pulled one, two, three times in Merrick's direction.

Present

The weather became angrier as rain clouds covered the entire sky. Goosebumps formed on patches of the regular skin I had left. I blended in with the nature around me, and so did Zekiel to a certain extent. There was discomfort in the way he walked around like he was hiding something horrid. His eyes would be intently fixated on the ground or at his feet—but never up ahead. I tried to not pry at him for a further explanation at what was going on. He was the type of person who savored any ounce of personal space he could get. *Respect boundaries.* Soft rumbles of thunder started. Colorful plants swayed back and forth in the wind, which made it feel as though the planet was breathing too. I tried to pull off the moss and growths from my body, but doing so only brought pain with no relief. *Will I ever get to reverse being morphed? I have to wish for this curse to go away.*

While leaving the entrance of the jungle, we suddenly came across a tall man who was breathing heavily. He was clearly set on a mission based on the tenseness of his expression. We walked directly into him like our paths were meant to cross for some reason. *How many people are here?* His black hair sprawled over his forehead messily and eyes were full of perseverance. Zekiel and I stopped in our tracks upon seeing him as he did the same. None of us spoke for a few moments. *He isn't looking at me at all... he's looking at—*

"Zekiel." the man spoke loudly.

"Nero." Zekiel responded.

I could tell that this was not a happy reunion. Nero stood up a bit taller while Zekiel hunched down slightly, both wound up while trying to figure out what to say next.

"Who are you?" Nero asked me.

"I'm Jameson." I stepped forward and shook his hand. "Nice to meet you."

"You've been taken here too? Ugh. How long was I in that time-consuming void for?" Nero walked up to Zekiel with his head held high as he spoke to him, "So. You also managed to escape from that place?"

Zekiel stared at the holes in his tattered boots. "I didn't 'escape'. Something… or someone… took me out of it." He spoke his words unsteadily in a spaced out manner.

"Well we should be thanking them, right?" Nero snickered and roughly smacked Zekiel's arm. "Why don't you look up? How can you ever see where you're going if you aren't paying attention to your path?"

"I don't need to take advice from you." Zekiel finally made eye contact with him and squared his shoulders. "I will never care what you have to say, Nero. I know what you've done. I'm aware of the type of person you are."

There were two major divides: one between Zayika against Anon and Amira… and a second involving Nero and Zekiel. I stepped a few paces away from them to create distance. I wasn't sure what they were referring to. *Stay cautious.*

"I'm not some kind of monster." Nero's voice was harrowing like the thunder he was talking over. "I ousted Saige because I was playing the game, Zekiel. I did what I needed to in order to survive. Everyone has to look out for themselves as they walk along the ground we are standing on. Go ahead and judge me. You will never know who I really am."

Zekiel's palms started to light up with flames as he got closer to his enemy. "You shouldn't have murdered her. Call it what it really was. Murder."

What happened with Yestin was an accident. Zekiel doesn't seem malicious, right?

"Oh come on. Like you really care that she is gone. You didn't love her. Stop pretending that I've taken away your soulmate." Nero sent a strong gust of wind from his palms and that, mixed with raindrops, got rid of the fire promptly. "I could hurt you right now for what you did to me, removing my wings and opening up that portal, but I won't. You know why? Because even though it resulted in misfortune for me… you did what you needed to in order to play the game. I respect that. I will commend those that operate by the rules."

"Do you even listen to yourself speak? It's nauseating!" Zekiel yelled out at him and used an immense amount of force to shove him backwards. "What about Saylor? How were you following any rules at all by killing her? You slit her throat open! You deserved to have both your wings taken away!"

Nero walked around in a circle a few times before responding. Large scars on his back shone under the morning sunlight as droplets of rain fell on them. He ran his fingers through his hair and laughed. *Why does his tongue look like that?* There were large groove marks so deep in his tongue that it seemed to be only hanging on by a thread. *Seems as if he almost bit it out…*

"I wasn't thinking when I killed her." Nero put his hands out in front of him. "I acted based on my emotions, which was foolish. I was the second person to be taken to this planet. Do you know how long I waited for others to arrive?"

"Becoming stir crazy isn't a valid excuse for cold-blooded murder. That doesn't justify your actions."

"I know it doesn't, but maybe it can help explain them to a certain degree. I met Gebu when I first arrived. He was my first friend here. We both waited hour after hour and felt each day pass by with nothing to do. I practiced using my abilities at the Over Ground faction as he cheered me on. He only had small wings given to him after being morphed, no abilities at all, but he would help me train for the fight we were told was coming soon. Despite this... I started to lose my edge over time. I became desperate to move forwards and get the ceremony started."

"Where is Gebu now?" Zekiel asked with crossed arms.

"I don't know." Nero's eyes looked worrisome for a moment. "Maybe he made it back to Earth somehow while we were in the void. Being more realistic though... he's probably dead. He couldn't fight even if it meant getting all of the riches in the world. He'd always talk about what he wanted in life, but I knew he didn't have it in him to put in the work required to earn it."

"Why should I care about any of this? I find it hard to believe that you were friends with anyone here, Nero. You came out of nowhere to our Land Dweller's faction and started attacking us. You blew up some of my people and then killed Saige as well. You don't deserve to be forgiven."

So this is the person who killed the woman that Zekiel was talking to in the jungle. Why would he? Raindrops fell down harder. They dripped into my eyes and fell over my mouth as I watched the exchange with an invested stare. *This doesn't sound like a case of Nero protecting himself, but instead... killing for sport.*

Nero punched the air and then fell down to rest on his knees. "Damn it, Zekiel, why am I even trying to explain myself to you? I lost a bit of my head when waiting for everyone else to spawn on the starting hills. I wasn't thinking clearly. When I took out those three at the beginning of this all... I felt different afterwards. My stomach turned. I realized that I needed to play with the intent to win what I deserved. Reckless actions only result in sickness afterwards."

"Do you still feel sick about it now?" I chimed in, feeling as though I gathered enough information to insert myself into their discussion.

Nero seemed pleased with my question and stood up to answer, "I don't feel sick anymore, Jameson. You know why?" His brown eyes looked at Zekiel as he asked me what was on his mind, "Do you believe in karma?"

That's easy to answer. "I do."

"So do I." Zekiel said through gritted teeth.

"Great. Maybe you will understand this, then. I was dealt out the karma I deserved. I took those two lives and then Saylor sawed off my wing. That painful removal was my consequence for the first Land Dweller I killed... and then, Zekiel, you taking off the second one was what I deserved for the other." Nero shuddered. "I can't describe in words how badly that hurt. I still have phantom pain that has never fully gone away from where they were."

Zekiel slicked his blonde hair away from his eyes. "When did karma come around for you killing Saylor then?"

"The void was my punishment. I hated it there. It was torture to be trapped in my mind."

"I didn't have the same experience." Zekiel seemed confused.

"Must've been nice." Nero looked at me for some reason. "I've paid my debts. I deserve to get back to Earth now."

"What about Saige? What was your consequence for murdering her?" Zekiel's voice cracked as he asked.

He must feel guilty about the accident with Yestin... I can sense it.

"I'll say this one last time. I took her life to get her wish. I played the game's rules like many others did here." Nero cracked his knuckles. "So let me ask you one last question, Zekiel, that I've been dying to get the answer to."

"What is it?"

I jolted my attention back and forth rapidly depending on who was speaking. *Where is this going?*

"That night in the jungle, when the knife hit Saige, where were you coming back from? We ran into each other quite close to where we are now actually. What were you doing out in the night so late with retribution swirling in your eyes?"

"I was going to..." Zekiel took a drawn out pause. "I went out to get Anon's wish."

"There we go. You aren't so perfect yourself after all, are you?" Nero patted Zekiel's shoulder and nodded. "We both did what was required to survive. That was our intent."

"But your blade was pointed at me. Saige stepped in front of it." Zekiel started to get distraught again with a clenched jaw. "You planned on killing me, not her."

"You're wrong." Nero's words sprung out of his mouth quickly. "I knew it wouldn't kill you. Anyone could see how much she loved you. It was painful. I already foresaw her jumping in front of you to take the knife.

That was called strategizing, playing by the rulebook, and using perception."

Zekiel was left speechless and some of his previously hidden emotions were crossing his features. His conversation with Nero consisted of the most words I'd ever heard him say since we met. *We need to get back on track with our plan.* I didn't want to get into a tangled mess with the others, but I could understand Zayika's and Zekiel's reasons behind their hostility... *Are Anon and Amira right in their own way? It seems clear that Nero isn't.* I liked the idea of playing by the rules in order to escape this planet filled with madness, but I wasn't on board with enabling someone who seemed to act without thinking at all about the others around them. *Every single one of our decisions will impact those around us, whether we like it or not. Life is not a game. We all have to give and get what we deserve.*

"Where do we go from here?" I asked Zekiel. "You know, with what we were discussing?"

"We resume our plan."

"You have a 'plan'?" Nero raised his eyebrows. "Can I hear it?"

"No." Zekiel scowled. "It doesn't involve you." He walked past him and shoved Nero aside as I trailed behind.

"Good luck on your endeavors, Nero." I said with a subtle hint of sarcasm behind my words as I went onwards through the rainfall. "Take care of yourself."

Thunder crashed again.

"Don't worry. I will." Nero replied as he took off in the opposite direction from where we were going in a way that made it seem as if he had a plan of his own.

CHAPTER EIGHT: ALREADY SEEN

Zekiel

Present

I lied to Jameson about a part of my plan. My deep-rooted intentions and personal choices were none of his business. I didn't need him to worry about me and be concerned with things he might not understand. He was a kind man that thankfully agreed to the idea I shared — that all we needed to do was get rid of Anon's wings, push Zayika in the void, and use the wish he was given to get back to Earth. The plan was solid and I was proud of myself for being able to think of it on such short notice with limited information. I wasn't emotionally attached to any of the three that I started my journey with. Zayika. Anon. Amira. I was not focused on what they were doing or feeling, but I was obligated to involve them in order to get sent back... to the void.

Going back to Earth was unimportant. I had no desire to be sent to my previous life where nothing was waiting for me besides haunting memories of the past. The only deviation I shared with Jameson about my plan was the part where I return to Earth with him. I didn't want that.

The plan in the back of my mind was to get rid of Anon's wings, open the portal, and simply get back into it. The fate of the others was not on my radar. I did not want to put Zayika in the void or participate in Jameson's wish, though I knew that my chances of success would be far greater if I kept my new acquaintance on board with the plan I devised for him.

I was fine with removing Anon's wings, which seemed to be miniscule in the grand scheme of things since in the past I had plotted to end his life. There used to be a great longing within me for getting a wish, but after experiencing the sheer freedom and peace of where I was taken, I didn't care about them anymore. The discovery of what it was like to be away from the disturbance and devastation that life could bring caused that. *Get back to peacefulness.* Anon losing his wings would be a small sacrifice for him to pay. I felt much better about taking that from him instead of issuing him a death sentence. *I can get back to the void. I have to be patient, mindful of the words I choose, and how much I let Jameson and the others know.*

Six Years Before

Zekiel put his arm around Jasmine as they sat across from Saige at a busy restaurant. It was a warm evening as the two celebrated her work interview together and interrogated their friend to see how it went.

"I'm not sure they'll pick me." Saige looked down into her cup of water and fiddled with the plastic straw in it.

"I think they will." Jasmine said supportively. "You have a lot to offer."

"Really?" Saige looked at Zekiel as she asked, searching his eyes for reassurance instead.

"Yeah, you do." He leaned the side of his head down onto Jasmine's.

Saige refrained from making eye contact with them for a few moments before responding, "I have a feeling that it's not going to happen."

Jasmine leaned slightly over the table. "You're a trustworthy person and one of the most loyal friends I've ever had. I was so lucky to meet you after Zekiel and I got together." He smiled and she continued, "If anything ever happens to me, I want you to promise to take care of him."

Saige sat up straight. "Why would you say something like tha—"

"Please don't say those types of things." Zekiel interjected.

"Both of you calm down. I'm just saying that I am glad to know that my boyfriend will be left in good hands if something goes wrong. You can't predict what will happen in the future."

Zekiel turned towards Jasmine and took both of her hands in his. "Everything will end up being okay. I'm sorry, but I can't listen to you speak that way. I'm going to try my best to take care of us, alright? If something happens to you... I'll be by your side. We're going to have a peaceful future."

From the corner of his eye he could see Saige anxiously swirling her straw around in circles while looking directly at him.

"Okay. Yeah, we will be okay." Jasmine lifted her drink in the air and prompted the other two to do the same. "Here's to a peaceful future!"

Present

Jameson and I luckily ran into Amira while on our way to find her and Anon. She was badly burnt on both of her arms and desperately trying to get away from something or someone. Her eyes met mine and she froze. It was surreal seeing someone I used to know again… and alive in front of me. Reality felt like an illusion. A lot of time passed since we'd spoken and I was reminded of the talk we had under trees after she joined our group. *I tried to warn her. I always knew that something bad would happen here.* I could tell that the two of us were unsure of what to say. *Where is Anon? Has something happened to him?* I tried to brace myself for unsettling news from her. *Don't tell me that he's gotten himself killed by being incautious. Hopefully Amira is the one making most of the decisions.* Once I snapped out of being surprised, I hurriedly tried to get answers.

"Why are you hurt?" I asked.

"We were on our way to find you and Anon." Jameson elaborated.

Amira stepped closer towards where we stood and winced at her cracking skin. "Zayika attacked us near the ocean after we left the courtyard. She separated Anon and me, and I have no clue where he is now. I just know he went in the opposite direction that I've come from and she's somewhere in the middle."

"Alright. We need to get you up to speed on our plan out of here." Jameson responded. "It seems like we don't have much time to catch up."

"We don't." Amira said. "Are you still experimenting with that grenade launcher?"

He laughed nervously. "I'm not sure why I aimed it at you guys. I was getting carried away, it's like Zayika put some sort of spell on me or something."

"I wouldn't be surprised if she did. Don't worry about it right now. We need to stay focused on other things." Amira replied dismissively and then smiled at me. "I'm happy to see you again, Zekiel, I'm glad that you are doing okay."

"Thanks."

I'm not 'doing okay'.

"Are you going to be alright?" Jameson asked Amira.

"I'll be alright. Zayika is going to have to do a lot worse if she wants me gone." She stood confidently. "I can join you both and hear about your plan along the way. We need to try to find Anon."

I nodded and started to lead us onwards. "We shouldn't waste any more morning light by just standing here. Let's go."

The three of us left and got closer to the broken castle that once was the Over Ground's faction. Amira's words revealed to me that the plan I developed was already in motion. There wasn't time to strategize further. We needed to get done what we sought out to do.

"I'm sorry she hurt you." I said to Amira.

"Don't apologize. I'm not surprised she did this... her mind is deteriorating. I've sensed this part of her ever since the two of us spoke on that old canoe when we were getting to know each other." Amira then looked at Jameson. "I need to talk to you about something. I know that you had a dream, but how exactly did you get here? You shouldn't have been able to."

"What does that mean?" He gave her a troubled look.

"To this planet. Eunoia. I don't know how you got here. I destroyed the waterfall—" Amira's eyes were frantic as we heard Zayika's voice booming in the sky.

"I can't tell what she's saying." I stated while trying to make sense of her words.

"Neither can I." Jameson chimed in. "Amira, I honestly don't know how I got here. I was dreaming and woke up in this place. That's it."

"Do you remember what happened in your dream?"

"Nothing. Everything was pitch black until a bright light appeared to jolt me awake after the pain and then I saw endless hills."

We have to keep Jameson and his wish safe. We also need to keep Anon's wings intact. I can't miss my opportunity to return to the void.

Zayika's voice echoed in the distance and it became easier to hear what she was saying. Her words consisted of taunts and menacing laughter that informed us how we wouldn't be able to 'hide for long'.

"Don't worry, Amira. Zekiel and I met earlier and found a way out of this. We also fought a giant crocodile, but that's a story we can share after we get out of here." Jameson tried to comfort her. "Let's find a better hiding space. We need to go somewhere near that floating castle and we will explain everything. Anon may have circled over to that area."

Amira won't hear my side of the plan, only Jameson's.

"Okay. I'd like to know what you've both thought of. Zayika is pretty much unstoppable."

"There seems to be a loophole." Jameson patiently informed her.

I tensed up. *He has no idea about me wanting to escape to the void. I have to calm down.* Fire started to briefly escape my palms again. I tried to slap away the small flames.

"Are you okay?" Amira asked me.

"Don't worry about it." I grunted and didn't look her way.

"Our plan is solid." Jameson continued, "I really believe it can work."

"That sounds great, but..." Amira seemed greatly concerned. "Do you mind if Zekiel and I speak alone in private for just a few moments?"

What does she need to say to me?

"Of course. No problem." Jameson responded as he stepped off to the side. "I'll be over here when the two of you are ready to continue."

Amira lowered her voice, "Hey Zekiel."

I nodded.

"I can't help but notice that something seems to be troubling you, are you alright? I heard from Anon that you disappeared somewhere on the planet. How did you make it out?"

It's nice of her to care.

"I'm not exactly sure where I was, or how I'm here now. I have more questions in my head than answers." I took a drawn out breath. "There's a lot on my mind."

"Do you want to talk about it?"

"I'm not sure."

"Well I'm around if you'd like to."

Amira started to walk away and an urge overcame me to let her know what was going on. *Maybe I should try to talk to her. She heard me out at the start of this journey and didn't turn against me. How much can I share?* "I get asked that often... if I am alright."

"I can't say I'm shocked. You're very quiet." Amira turned around to face me again. "Ever since we've met I've sensed unease within you."

"Really?"

"Yeah. I'm very sorry that you lost Saige. I know you two were close."

"She was one of my greatest friends." I brushed my hair aside to make full eye contact and wanted to focus on something else. "Sorry. I'm not quite ready to speak about her death."

"That's alright and completely understandable. What else is going on?"

I tried to find the best words to get my feelings across. "Amira, do you remember what it was like when you lost your innocence? Either out of curiosity or having it ripped away by someone else?"

She looked at me intensely. "Yes. Vividly."

"Me too." I continued. "I've lost many people and a lot of hope during my life. I'll be honest with you... there is not a lot of life left in me."

"Are you hurt? You aren't close to death, right? I see the wound on your le—"

"No. Not physically. I've been feeling dead on the inside for a while now."

Amira gave me a non-judgmental glance as she placed both hands behind her back. "When did this start? What would help you feel better?"

"It has festered over time. I'm exhausted. There was one moment a long time ago when I discovered what death was. Being so young, I couldn't wrap my head around it. Later on I learned more about what it really means to die."

Amira was silent.

"My head feels contaminated with doubt. I don't know where I'm going to go once my life ends. I'm unsure of what's waiting for me on the other side."

"I see. Uncertainty is unraveling you." She shook her head. "Zekiel, I know that there is light and victory that's waiting for us. That sounds vague, but my intuition tells me that we will end up out of harm's way."

I was surprised at her response. "Who is 'we'?"

"Us who were brought here to Eunoia."

"I hope you are right." I told her. "What really happened when I was gone? Who won the final wishes?"

"Anon and I did." She seemed to be fighting off a layer of grief in her words, "We didn't take Zayika to Earth. She found a way to bring us back here to get her revenge. Everyone else died in the closing fights."

"I'm assuming that you hunted others from different factions then? What was it like ending their lives?"

Amira's eyes searched my face. "Are you asking me this out of judgement? Or because of something else?"

Don't speak about Yestin. "Forget it." I tossed a hand up in the air. "But can I ask why you didn't save Zayika? I'm not judging. I know what it's like to keep an eye out for those who mean the most to you, but is there a deeper reason for the choices you both made together?"

"Anon saved my life and asked for us both to be taken back home." Amira always smiled when saying his name. "Since he had that covered, I focused on destroying the waterfall where I was kidnapped."

Wait... "You were able to leave this planet with his wish?" *Saige and I could have just used hers alone? I didn't have to go hunt down Anon at all?*

"Yes. He asked for me to return alongside him."

"Oh." *She wouldn't have died that night if I didn't leave her behind.*

"Why?" Amira saw how distressed I had become. "What makes you ask?"

"It's nothing." *How am I supposed to tell her that I sought to kill the man she's always adored? I have to change the topic.* "Neither of you really said anything for Zayika? She was left here to roam the planet alone with the representatives, I assume?"

"Exactly."

"I would've used wishes similarly with Saige if I had known I could do that. She always looked out for me, and I wish that my head was on the right way so I could have done the same for her in the end."

"You didn't answer my earlier question." Amira stated calmly. "What could help you feel better?"

Retreat. I've said enough. "I'm not sure, but I think we should continue onwards, getting back home will help me tremendously." *She doesn't need to know where my home is now.*

"Alright." Amira was hesitant to let go of our conversation but recognized my conversational boundaries. "Jameson, are you ready to go on?" she called out.

"Of course." He rejoined us.

I trailed behind the two as they got to know each other and kicked at mounds of dirt. *Keep quiet.* Habitually I withdrew my true thoughts and feelings from those around me, unless we were very close, which was a rare instance. *My plan will be successful, this is what I am sure of. I will find a way to get back to where I belong.* The conversation with Nero had left me shaken to my core. I was profoundly frustrated at how he explained and justified his heinous acts. The two of us were both trying to look out for ourselves and didn't see eye to eye. Some of the points he made became stressors that I couldn't stop thinking about. *I went to hunt down Anon for his wish as he did the same for Saige... Can I really justify these feelings of disdain towards him entirely?* Him killing Saylor and other Land Dwellers was unforgivable, he lost his wings and entered the void, but that wasn't enough of a punishment. Their lives were stolen for no reason at all. Nero clearly wrestled with lack of common sense and self-control. *Does he deserve to still have his life after taking theirs? I don't think so. But I can't let it eat away at me.*

Though Nero and I were different, I couldn't add further fuel to the flames I had to suppress when I thought about his actions. Memories compounded in my mind. The things I'd observed and felt made me sick like an untreatable disease. My only escape was, up until entering the void, the nights when I would be able to get some sleep. Not speaking about issues helped them almost disappear. It wasn't until I found the planet's void that I experienced what it was like for them to be gone completely. That was escapism to the most extreme degree possible. *Stick by Jameson, Amira, and Anon. Nero can't distract me from the bigger picture — he has his own agenda and so do I.*

It was unnecessary to tell the others about my plan to re-enter through the portal I was once forced into. *They won't understand my reasoning. I'll only call attention to myself. What if one of them tries to stop me? They probably think that the void is an awful place filled with torture and crushing darkness...* It was odd how Nero experienced that place in an opposite way to me. *The planet speaks to us all differently, doesn't it?* Even from the early start on the hills I knew all our minds and aspirations were vastly different from one another. It seemed more logical to look out for my own self instead of forming temporary friendships and romantic relationships. My lifelong friend was called here too when she awoke beside me on the hills. *It's time now to go on alone.*

Everything was wrong. Brutality. Unfairness. Regret. But the void? Nothing hurt in the void. Nothing was coming after me there. I couldn't see, feel, or hear anything destructive. My loyalty when brought to the planet was to Saige and the others also placed in the Land Dweller faction. All of my group members were killed, and I let my friend down tremendously. *Look out for myself… no one else that matters is left.* Jameson was chosen to be in the same faction as me, so I stayed alongside him for as long as I could. We formulated a plan with two sides to it. I presented it to him but in a manner that kept a part of it only known to myself — like I was holding an unturned coin.

Jameson still didn't have a clue about my intentions to disappear. *If he found out, would he care? Try to stop me? Or actually let my life and choices be my own without interfering?* Either way, I didn't want to risk it. We had only just met and I felt that no one else knew me well enough to have a suspicion of what I wanted. The only person who would've been able to sense what I longed for here was dead. *Saige, rest softly. I wish you knew that staying close to me would only end in tragedy.* Past forced friendly glances and misleading words to Amira and Jameson, there was a truth that remained permanently embedded in my mind: *I have to look out for myself and get to where I belong.*

CHAPTER NINE: BUTTERFLY EFFECT

Amira

Present

I finished listening to Jameson's and Zekiel's plan and was impressed. There seemed to be at least one possibility of outsmarting Zayika. *She's so wrapped up in the goal of ruining us, I'm sure she hasn't thought of the possibility of us sending her into the void.* I tried to remain hopeful that every step of the plan would not be interrupted or ruined by an unforeseeable obstacle. Zayika burning me ended up solidifying all of the unsympathetic feelings I had towards her. There was no excuse for tormenting others the way she did. No valid reason could be found for why she tried to manipulate the narrative and make it seem as though she was the victim. She had a narrow view of the meaning of revenge, a view that only explored her own perspective and not mine or Anon's. She wanted to be catered to. Zayika was enjoying every second of making it seem as though we were the ones who did the wrong thing. Somehow, she couldn't hear her own maniacal laughter or see how needless the brutality that she inflicted was. My skin stung like a salted wound as I tried to ignore the feeling.

Use this pain as fuel. Let her throw her punches at us, but make sure she misses. She will only make the rest of us stronger as we come together.

There was a part of me which felt like our strategy was a bit too simple, that it would be easier said than done, but I suppressed those thoughts and focused on one crucial part of it all... *Anon's wings. Will he be able to give them up?* I didn't want to doubt the person who I had so much faith in, but there were times when he could be stubborn during tense circumstances. *Please, Anon, be the integral part of this journey like you've always wanted and do this for us. Face the pain.* I thought a lot about him before we finally crossed paths again.

It was reassuring to look back on the past we shared together and realizing what we could live through. The two of us were able to fight and proved our capabilities in the past. We needed to communicate more than ever before. Our previous talks on the beach used to have casual undertones where we could be playful and forget about the arena we were in. But this time? We couldn't afford to let our guard down that way. Anon wanted to keep us away from Zayika's view, but we needed to take more action than that. We eventually found him hiding on the ground near some cover.

"Hey!" I called out while running to him.

Anon sprang up and met me halfway to pull me into a tight embrace. "Hey."

It felt like everything was going to be okay in that moment as my lips met his. *I'm so glad he's here.* We both smiled as we kissed for the first time and gently held onto each other.

"Are you alright? Have you faced Zayika again since we've been separated?"

"I'm okay. And no, thankfully I haven't." he smiled.

"Um..." Zekiel interrupted us awkwardly.

"Wow." Anon stepped closer to his former acquaintance. "Zekiel. Haven't seen you in a while."

"That is true." he responded and then looked at me. "It's nice to see that you both still have each other. I'm betting that the four of us here will make a pretty good group for tricking Zayika."

"I hope so." Jameson joined the conversation. "She tried to get me to side with her."

Anon bit his lip and charged forwards. "I didn't forget about that, by the way, how you tried to blow up Amira and me!"

"I'm not sure what happened. It was odd." Jameson stood his ground. "But it seems like you want more of what took place back there by how you are coming at me."

"I don't. I just need you to understand that you can't fire at us and assume we will forgive and forget right away."

I stepped in between the two of them to settle things down. "I've already forgiven him."

Anon gave me a distressed look. "Seriously? How?"

"Because I believe what he's saying. It's obvious that Zayika has some powers that we will never understand. Anon, she got us back here by pulling strings, you don't think that she can make things that are out of the ordinary happen? That she won't manipulate others? Please let it go and forget what happened."

"Fine." he said to me and glared at Jameson while his scars flickered lightly. "Don't do that ever again."

"What happened to your arms? They look different now." Zekiel asked Anon coldly, like he was only taking interest in order to distract himself from something else.

"I was struck by my own lightning." He looked down at his arms. "Worst thing I've ever felt. What happened to your leg?"

"A massive crocodile took a piece out of it."

"He cauterized the wound himself, it was crazy!" Jameson said exuberantly.

Anon turned to face me and laughed. "There is an abnormal crocodile and anglerfish on this planet… but why is it that a person is much more threatening?"

"Humans are always more dangerous than creatures." I stated in a serious tone. "I've seen it firsthand."

I need to speak in private with Anon about this plan. He deserves to have an initial reaction away from the other two. He has to be on board with getting his wings torn off.

"So where do we go from here?" Anon asked all of us with glistening eyes.

Jameson stepped forwards, "Well, we devised a plan that invo—"

I quickly cut him off. "I'd like to briefly talk to Anon about it alone, if that's okay with both of you?"

Zekiel and Jameson agreed to give us time and stayed behind while I called Hippo out from her dwelling place. I was thankful to have more alone time with my favorite person on Eunoia. I fought off anxiety about telling Anon the plan, but I was especially thankful that we at least bought some time away from Zayika to strategize and figure out what steps to take next. The ocean on Eunoia was similar to Earth's as it stretched for miles and miles with a large percentage of it being undiscovered. Since Anon was unable to go underneath it with me for a suspended period of time, I commanded Hippo to bring us out to a faraway spot while resting on her for a much needed conversation. The two of us tried to settle down as well as we could even though it was difficult knowing in the back of our minds that Zayika was somewhere searching for us... or even worse... patiently waiting for us to come to her.

Anon solemnly looked at the skin of mine that was burned. "I can't believe she did this to you."

"I'll be okay. We have to stay strong despite the attacks she's thrown at us so far."

"What are we going to do?" he asked. "We need to finish this once and for all. I'm tired of hearing her voice."

I admired his newfound drive to get things done. "You're right. While you were fending for yourself against her, I ran into Zekiel and Jameson. When the two met each other they devised a plan to get us four off the planet. It's an approach that would eliminate Zayika and let the rest of us go home."

"Really? That sounds unbelievable." Anon dipped his hand into the multicolored water.

"I know it does, but think about it, the four of us could get Zayika cornered. We all have our own abilities to use against her. While you, Jameson, and I are attacking her, you could... allow Zekiel to get rid of both your wings. This would catch her off guard as we force her into the portal that will open while making sure you stay out of it. Once she disappears, we'll use Jameson's wish to ask the remaining Over Grounds representative to send us all back to Earth—this time with no abilities."

"Wait, what?" He looked at me like I was mad. "I think we need to focus on the part where you want my wings to get torn off."

I sighed. "No. I don't want them to be, I just think that it's the best way to get out of this situation. Zayika is not easy to bring down. There needs to be sacrifice."

"Why can't you sacrifice something then? Why does it have to be me?" Anon's face was filled with frustration. "Do I have to fear you too?"

"What are you talking about?" I moved a bit closer and he pushed himself backwards. "There's no way for me to open the portal, you know this."

"Why are you acting so nonchalant about me getting maimed? It will be torture! What if the plan doesn't work?" He started to spiral. "What if I bleed out and die from it? Who will heal me?"

I thought quickly. *Calm him down.* "Zekiel could cauterize the wound." I presented the idea peacefully.

"Amira, what is wrong with you right now?" Anon slouched as he spoke. "It's like you're not thinking at all about how I will feel. Cauterization isn't something to throw around like it's painless and easy."

"Of course it won't be for you."

"What does that mean? Are you saying I'm weak?"

"No. Anon." *He's flipping my words around. Choose them carefully.* "You aren't weak. If you were then we wouldn't still be alive and talking to one another right now. I'm just saying that it would be hard for anyone, but I think you can handle it. We don't have many options. We need that portal to reopen again and get Zayika inside of it. The representative is able to grant Jameson's wish. Let's use it and go back home just like we were always meant to."

Anon scoffed. "You know what? How about I propose a brand new plan? Let's keep hiding from Zayika and secure our fate with his wish then. Leave the maniac completely out of it. I'm tired of dealing with her, exhausted actually, and right now... I'm not feeling too fond of yo—"

"Really?" I backed away further from him too. "You're going to turn on me now? When I need you the most? Anon, you have to think critically. In a perfect world we could pursue your plan, but I don't believe Zayika will allow that to happen. She's more powerful than anyone else here. I think you need to have more of an open mind if you want us to live through this."

"A-alright. I'll think about your idea." He stumbled over his words and already seemed to regretfully repair the tense air.

"I'm not trying to be overly blunt or harsh with you. You have to think about where I've come from. I've witnessed crime scenes that I'll never forget. There are places I've memorized in excruciating detail. Blood stains. Body parts. Shattered items."

"Why are you saying this to me? Why relive it again in a conversation if you don't have to?" Anon wouldn't look me in the eye.

"Because. When I was kidnapped at the waterfall... it impacted my mind. It was such an awful experience, not just being strangled, but everything about that eerie night. Every time I close my eyes I can hear the rushing wind again and see the trees blowing back and forth around me as if they were all waving goodbye to my presence."

He started to take me more seriously. "How does that tie into right now?"

"The weather was similar to the storm brewing around us here. That man and his ill intentions are very reminiscent of our former teammate that we are dealing with now."

"Oh… I guess that makes sense."

"On Earth I know that we tried to refrain from talking about this place, but I need to right now." I glanced upwards at the purple sky and took Anon's hand in mine. "You want to know two other things that I'll never forget from this experience?"

"What?" he finally looked at me again as he responded.

"The first would be when I met Hippo." I put my other hand on top of my anglerfish that was supporting us above the waves. "It's hard to describe what it was like so deep underwater and being brought to her."

"When you were morphed?"

"Yes. You saw when I was captured off the canoe and dragged downwards… but I've never told you about what happened there. I was morphed at the Oceanic Guardian's castle and woke up with the ability to breathe underwater."

"That must feel odd, scary even."

"It was at first, but it's something I got used to doing." I paused. "Hippo was in front of me when I woke up. She pulled me to her in a current while I was resting. I remember my eyes opening and feeling my stomach drop as I realized how deep down in the waters I really was. There was nothing but pure darkness in my peripheral vision and the only thing in focus was Hippo's giant teeth illuminated by the glowing orb behind me. Her glossy eyes silently told me that everything taking place was meant to happen."

"My morphing experience wasn't like that." Anon shuddered a bit. "We can talk about that later though. What is your second favorite memory?"

"Meeting you, of course." I said steadily and with no doubt in my mind. "The feeling of loneliness while running on top of the starting hills was practically unbearable. Anon, I was horrified. I wanted to wake up from what I thought was a dream so badly. I overcame many mental hurdles just to climb on top of the next hill in front of me. The challenge paid off when the five of you came into my view."

He smiled. "Really?"

"You stood out the most. You always have." I continued, "The others could never see what I notice in you. Us meeting was meant to happen. I think that the two of us were called here to solve this mystery and to make the other better."

Anon placed his other hand on top of mine and leaned towards me. "I'm not sure I deserve someone like you. I'm sorry for my failures, I really am, I jus—"

"You don't have to say those things." I told him.

"I'm trying to use my words, Amira, but they're failing me. I want to apologize for my shortcomings."

"Do it with your actions then." My eyes were pleading for his cooperation. "If you have to, please sacrifice your wings. I'll make sure we take care of any bleeding. I just need you to do whatever you can."

"Okay." He sighed. "It's going to hurt to have them removed. Getting them was an awful experience, so I can't imagine the pain of both being torn out."

"I'm not sure there's any other way to win. Zayika is too strong. Anything we use against her will end up being reversed."

"Yeah. Good point."

We both looked over the lightning bolt scars left all over his skin and then at the burn marks on mine.

"We can't defeat someone that has the type of power she possesses." I reiterated.

"I'm glad that Jameson arrived. Even though we both are technically Wish Carriers… I'm not sure we could use our wishes a second time. Did you happen to read anything about that on the stone at sea?"

I shook my head. "No, but I assume we'd be out of luck. Let's make sure we defend Jameson at all costs. Zayika could very easily see through this plan and eliminate him if he's no use to her before finishing off the two of us and Zekiel. I believe the only reason why she hasn't taken him out yet is because she thinks he will not turn against her by helping us."

Anon started to give a half-smile, but it soon vanished as he seemed to be reminded of a suppressed thought. "Amira. I found something out when I showed up here. Up until now I wasn't sure how to tell you because I don't know if it's that important."

"What?" I sat up beside him as Hippo still carried us in the harsh waves.

"You know that Nero is here too, right?"

I was confused at first. "Nero?"

"Yes. He was in my faction and was taken into the portal with Zekiel after his second wing was removed. You may have seen him briefly at the opening ceremony. He's not someone you should want to encounter. His only focus is to destroy anyone that gets in his way."

"Sounds like Zayika."

"He is sort of like her." Anon's eyebrows lifted. "Wow, I just realized that you never met him before he vanished. You're lucky."

"He's really that bad?"

"Nero is someone that could ruin everything. If my suspicions are correct… Zayika has already recruited him alongside her to enforce mass destruction upon the rest of us."

"What abilities does he have?"

"Well..." Anon's eyes were timid. "Now that his wings are gone, I believe he can only control wind and throw knives. He's gotten a lot of practice, so he won't be an easy target."

Hippo helped me take down enemy faction members and I felt confident enough to do whatever I needed to in order to maintain the safety of us who deserved it. "Simple or not, I think we can deal with him."

Anon glanced hopefully. "Really?"

"Yes. We'll just have to make sure Zayika is distracted, preferably by Jameson since she hasn't killed him and has no reason to if he doesn't reveal his alliance with us. He would be gone by now if that's what she wanted."

I could tell that Anon was trying to make sure Zayika wasn't hovering somewhere in the sky in a cloud of stars as he listened intently. "This sounds good. We should get Nero's whereabouts and have Jameson distract Zayika. After Nero is dead... the four of us will complete our goal."

"Exactly." I ran my fingers over his.

"Then we can go home and never come back here again."

I felt tenacity growing within me at his words. *I think we can actually do this.*

Six Weeks Before

Anon woke up Amira after she fell asleep on him in the backseat. "Hey. We're here."

She opened her eyes at his words and experienced the initial shock of realizing that they actually made it home.

Amira's tenseness grew as they unbuckled their seat belts. She was grinding her teeth without even realizing as they pulled up to the curbside.

"I'll go get your payment." Amira told the man up front. "Just give me a few minutes plea—"

"Ah." He turned around. "Don't worry about it, I can foot the bill. You two seem exhausted."

"You quite literally have no idea." Anon responded as he patted the driver's shoulder. "Thank you for what you've helped us with. Good karma will come for you."

"What in the world?" Amira's dad said from their front porch. He saw the taxi drive up from the living room window and came outside to see what was happening.

"Amira?" Her mom ran across the driveway and threw her arms over her daughter. "You are home! You're finally home!" She began crying hysterically.

"We have been looking for you for so many days... so many sleepless nights!" Her dad joined in, hugging Amira.

The three were holding one another as Anon shyly walked up to them from around the vehicle. He anxiously looked at his wings and scars while waiting to hear what they would say about them.

"Amira, who is this?" Her mom's attention turned to him. "Who's this young man with... wings?"

"There is a lot to explain. I'm not sure where to start." Amira took Anon's hand. "We have so much to tell you."

Her mother and father took them to the garden and made tea to sip on. It was a sunny afternoon and the air was full of burning questions that they couldn't wait to ask.

"I made posters of you." Amira's mom brought one outside from the dining table. "I put many up throughout town, eagerly waiting by our phone night and day hoping to get a call about your return."

"Where were you?" her dad asked in a lowered voice.

"Somewhere far away." Amira started to explain. "I was kidnapped at the waterfall while on a case with Arcadia."

"Something happened to it. It crumbled in on itself not too long ago, actually." Her mom hit her hands together. "I knew that job was a bad ide—"

"It wasn't the job—that sounds like a freak accident." her dad interrupted. "I've always been proud of you for taking on such great responsibility in your career, Amira, though I'm sorry and greatly frightened about how you were taken away. We've been so worried. I can hardly believe this."

"Who took you?" Her mom was shaking as she leaned forward to put an arm on Amira.

She shook her head tiredly while responding, "I don't know who it was. Someone at the waterfall had stalked and took me somewhere very far away from here. That's where I met—"

"Anon." He leaned forward from the bench to shake their hands. "My name is Anon. It's nice to meet you both. We met others and tried to survive together, to put it very simply."

"Explain the wings on your back." Her dad gave him a skeptical look. "Those are fake, right?"

"They're real. This is going to sound ridiculous, but they were given to me. We both were given… abilities and underwent physical changes. We had no idea where we were. There was danger everywhere. I met your daughter not too long after arriving and we've looked out for one another ever since."

An orange and blue colored butterfly flew onto the lip of Amira's tea mug. "Everything he said is true. It wasn't easy. Somehow we've made it back alive, though." She watched as the insect went back into the air and through the garden. "Let's all try to relax. Anon and I will walk you through what happened. This is a long story, but we're so grateful to be back and won't take this life for granted."

Present

"I saved Omar's life when we first showed up on the hills." Anon told me.

"Really?" I asked with undivided attention.

"Why do you seem so surprised?" He started to get defensive again.

"Because when I first met him he told me that you hadn't saved anyone else since you all showed up here."

"When did he say that?"

I let out a deep breath. "When you were out in the ocean trying to find out what the shining light was."

"Wow. That's surprising. I wonder why he would take it upon himself to make a comment like that."

"Yeah. I stood up for you in that moment, telling him maybe that was why you were risking your life for the rest of us."

"What was his reply?"

"Nothing. Omar was quiet and timid around me after that. He acted like I was about to catch him in a lie."

Everything was being pieced together.

"I wonder why he tried to paint me in a bad light at that time. We clashed for a while, which I'm sure you remember. Deep down my banter with him always felt friendly to a point." Anon shifted his focus on the rising and falling waters. "He was going through a lot. I don't think he liked the attention I was getting. I feel bad about what happened to him and the cards he was dealt."

My chest tightened as I watched Anon bite his lip and hold back tears.

"I'm sorry you watched him die. That was an awful moment." I put my hand on his again and spoke with care. "What happened to him wasn't your fault and I hope you know that."

"What if I got there in time? What if I used my wings like I should've and flew over to him? I didn't think fast enough! Why do I act quickly when I don't think something through? Amira, why did I fail? Why have I destroyed our wish and—"

"It's okay."

"N-no it's not. I failed myself." Anon closed his eyes. "I wanted to be a leader, but instead I've made everything fall apart! I'm the opposite of what this planet's meaning holds. My mind is not well. I even failed you. I should've used my wish to secure our future in a hopeful and healthy way. Instead I simply asked to get back to Earth with you. I wasn't mindful of everything that could go wrong. How are you not upset with me about this? I can hardly believe that you're not."

I moved my arms to hold onto him. "We can't change the past. Anon, you have to forgive yourself."

"How am I supposed to with Zayika constantly over my shoulder telling me everything that I don't want to hear or think about?"

Help him calm down.

"Do you remember what I said to you when you found Omar dead?"

"Yes. You said… 'you need to think clearly in order to survive right now'."

I smiled. "That statement remains just as true in this situation with Zayika." We leaned on each other. The bridges of our noses touched again. "Let's go back to the shore and find Omar's body. We should give him a burial. When we're done… we'll finally wake up from this nightmare that we have been forced into." *Stay strong. I have to stay strong for both of us.* Anon's mind was on the verge of breaking down, I had seen what that looked like once before… it was after enduring what he called the 'blue trance'. Allowing him to experience some closure was so important for the situation we were in.

I directed Hippo where she needed to go. The rain and wind wasn't letting up, but instead growing stronger with each minute that escaped us. *He needs to properly say goodbye to his friend.* I heard Anon swallowing a lump in his throat as we got closer to the destruction site of the Over Ground's castle. It was important for him to confront the past and finally let go of his guilt. *His heart isn't in the wrong place.* Zayika was trying to villainize us, and she made it very apparent. I disagreed with her constant guilt trips. I stood by my wish to destroy the waterfall, and also supported Anon in what he chose as well. We both decided to speak for what was in our hearts at the closing ceremony and Zayika couldn't accept that it didn't involve her. Her feelings were not our responsibility. I grew to love Anon and prioritized my needs and his over everything else. *There is no way we can ever please everyone. Anon and I need to stand by what he chose to do. Stay confident. If I have to fight Zayika then I will. We can outsmart her.* Life wasn't fair, ever, and that was a lesson that Zayika needed to learn.

"I know that he's over here." Anon's voice took me out of my thoughts as he pointed to a pile of rubble up ahead.

He pulled me into his arms and we flew off the top of Hippo to get to the sand. "Yes, this is where Omar fell."

We moved several rocks in order to get to what was left of his broken body. I put my hand up to my face at the sight of him. Anon paused for a moment before speaking; it was evident that he wanted to ask me something. I waited patiently in silence as rays of lightning could be seen in the sky. I remembered what it was like to come across him holding Omar. I would never forget his sobs of despair. *Leaving Zayika behind was fine, but... we should have asked for the others to be saved... right?* I fought off regret. Feeling guilty wasn't going to get us where we needed to go.

"How should we dig through the sand?" He hunched forwards with both palms on his knees while looking at our deceased friend.

"I have an idea." I called Hippo out of the water again and directed her to bite into a smaller piece of land off to our left. "Let's take him over to the side for a moment and give her enough room to pave the way."

Anon followed my instructions and we took Omar's body carefully into our hands. Where his head should have been was replaced with fragments of bone and flesh, and the rest of him had been decomposing. Hippo dashed forward and used her front teeth to bite into the planet with loud movements as she grunted.

"We'll have to hurry up a bit." Anon told me. "We've caught Zayika's attention."

I shrugged. "I'm sure she already knows where we are, and if not, we aren't too hard to find. She'll be coming after us sooner or later no matter what we do. We might as well take some time while burying him. If she wants to interrupt this moment... so be it. That would only reveal more about who she is." I tried to speak tenderly but also be firm in my resistance to succumb underneath Zayika's pressure.

"Okay."

We placed Omar down into the deep-set and freshly made grave for him. *Now you can rest properly. We never got to know each other well, but I always wanted you to make it and beat the odds that everyone seemed to put up against you.* Neither of us spoke while putting sand over him and Hippo watched with glossy eyes at what we were doing. It was as if she understood what was happening while staying on land for as long as possible to be present.

"Thanks for helping." I told her.

She let out an extended hum that sounded almost identical to a blue whale. Her cries echoed with sorrow as Anon put his hands behind his head and mentally prepared himself to say words for his friend's passing.

"Omar. I hope you are resting in peace. I never foresaw this happening back when we were around each other. I am sorry for letting you down and not being there to catch you again as I did in the beginning." He paused before concluding his closing thoughts, "I hope that your inner storms have subsided just as your art represented... and that you've found your sunset."

I kept my sentiments for him in my head and we stood together for just a few minutes until Zekiel and Jameson found us and made their way over. It was obvious what was taking place to them as they kept their voices quiet when approaching. Jameson stopped walking and stood quietly behind the rest of us as our estranged friend got closer.

"Who's down there?" Zekiel asked slowly.

"Omar." Anon replied.

"How and when did he die?"

"After you disappeared. Right before I used my wish with Amira to go home. There was a storm, quite similar to the one we're in right now, and it shook this planet to its core. Omar was up on a ledge of our faction working on his art and he fell. There was no time to save him."

Zekiel grimaced. "On a planet filled with others trying to kill each other, he managed to lose his life because of nature. I'm sorry to hear this. Him and I were never close, but he did try to help defend Saige and me when Nero attacked us in the jungle. He had good motives. There's not many of us left, are there?"

"No." I replied. "From our group of six we are now down to four."

"What about Nero?" Jameson spoke up.

"You had the pleasure of running into him? I envy you." Anon said sarcastically. "He didn't start this game alongside us. If he claims he did then he's lying. Don't trust him. All he brings around is negative energy and competitiveness."

"Remember, though, that we have to compete to survive." I said. "I can't speak for Nero since I've never met him, but if he's acting on a natural instinct of self-defense… I'm not sure I could blame him for that."

"You don't understand, Amira." He couldn't hold his tongue at my differing viewpoint. "Nero is someone that we need to stay away from. He's obnoxious and is only looking out for himself."

"Interesting." Jameson responded. "That's what Zayika says about you, Anon."

"Well she's wrong."

"Then what if you're wrong about him?"

"He's not." Zekiel came to his defense. "Just keep him out of our plans. We don't need him turning against us the first chance he gets."

Jameson dropped the topic. "Alright."

"Zayika says a lot of things, she likes to run her mouth." Anon looked at Jameson. "But that doesn't mean they are true. Make sure you are thinking for yourself. I think it's pretty obvious here who is in the wrong between us."

No one spoke as tension lingered in the air.

"Let's just forget about it." Jameson tried to calm Anon down. "I like to try picking my fights wisely."

"Brilliant." He turned to me. "Amira, can we talk for just one moment alone?"

"Yes."

"Just wait here for a couple minutes please." he said to Zekiel and Jameson.

"Only for a bit longer." Zekiel responded. "I get that you both want time together, but time is running out. If it's true that Zayika really is going to destroy everything in her path, if she's truly determined on her mission, we have to get ours into action."

"I know." Anon said impatiently. "There's just something I need to handle."

"Well then figure it out." Zekiel motioned at Jameson to walk away with him. "I'm not trying to be too harsh Anon, I don't enjoy confrontation, but you have a history of negligence combined with rash decision making. Get it together."

"Is everyone against me?" Anon asked under his breath, but I managed to hear him.

"I'm not." I put my hand on his back. "But that won't matter at all if we don't move along and expedite the plan we've put into place. Now, what is it you need to tell me?"

CHAPTER TEN: THE THUNDERSTORM

Anon

Present

I wanted to speed time up and get our battle with Zayika over with. Zekiel and Jameson thought of a way to end everything on Eunoia, but unfortunately it meant more suffering for me. *Why did I not ask for Zayika to be spared too? I bet she'll enjoy seeing my wings ripped off by Zekiel… if she doesn't do it before him.* I began to search the deep corners of my mind for answers that she desperately wanted to know. Something she told me earlier sparked a train of questions within me: *Why did I not ask for Omar to be brought back and come with us? And Saige? For even Zekiel to reappear?* My mind ruminated on the realization that I could have asked for anything, but I didn't, though I also didn't regret what I asked for. For the first time on the planet I felt as though others would listen to my voice and that there was power within it to decide how I wanted my life to go. Amira became the most important person to me after meeting her near the hills. Up until then I didn't feel cared about or respected by the other members of our group. She was always different in the best way possible. *I need to get myself together. I can't fail her too in this fight. Make her proud.*

She was magnetically charged with confidence and poise. There were many times when I'd seemed like a clumsy fool in comparison to her when she was beside me. It never mattered to me that we were placed into different factions. Those locations were not my home, but I felt at home when I was around her. I became desperate to get us back to Earth so that I could eventually build one with her there. She inspired me to put in continuous effort to be a leader for the others we met at the start. Zekiel, Saige, Omar, and Zayika... but things went awry. It felt like everything became cursed when Zayika saved my life out in the middle of the ocean. I remember thanking her for the heroic act and how she didn't accept that. *She never really cared about rescuing me, it's always been about rescuing her own self this entire time.* Her rough grip felt like a lethal needle as her nails plunged into my skin while yanking me out of the water, but when Amira held me afterwards it was like the venom was removed by her soft touch.

The spotlight Zayika placed onto my shortcomings and mistakes was only more poison in my mind. *I know that I'm right about her, but has she been right about me? Do I deserve all of this? Do I deserve to die at her hand?* Zayika's words replayed in my mind when she asked me to wish for her fate. I responded that I couldn't take both her and Amira. The representative never corrected me. *Was I right? Is Zayika wrong?* I needed a concrete answer. *I need to find out how messed up my actions have been.* I decided to track down the Over Grounds representative to find out the truth since there was no one else who could provide it. I decided to set out alone over the planet and told Amira to stay behind with Zekiel and Jameson. *This has to be done alone.* I longed for more time to think and reflect on my past and the choices I made. Amira was on standby waiting for me to tell her what was going on. I wasn't sure how she'd react.

"We're going to part ways for just a little while. There is something I need to do."

"Can I go with you?" Amira asked me.

"Not right now. I'm sorry."

The sky above was turning a dark shade of blue and the storm grew stronger as wind picked up and heavier raindrops began sprinkling over us. We both were freezing cold as the distance between where we stood kept growing. *I can't let her down. I chose her. For some reason… she chose me too. Don't fail this time.*

"Why not? What is it you're doing? Are you trying to take on Zayika alone? What about the plan?"

I grabbed Amira's hand and without a second thought I spoke, "I will be back. I will see you again. I just need answers."

"Why can't I go with you?"

"Because I don't know what's going to happen. I want you close to your fighting companion since I'm heading away from the ocean."

"But… you are my fighting companion."

"I want you near Hippo just in case. Stay with the other two for now, please, and when I come back we will face Zayika and finish this once and for all. There isn't much time left."

We kissed each other slowly and stood in silence for a few moments. I looked over my shoulder at the hills and thought of when I was first taken to Eunoia.

Seven Weeks Before

Anon woke up in the middle of several hill mounds that ranged in height and depth. He got up from the ground and rubbed the back of his head in confusion. After going over three hills he saw a woman not too far from him on a different hill. Her wavy silver and purple hair moved along with her quick footsteps. As he headed in her direction to speak to her, he noticed out of the corner of his eye that there were two other people on the hills to the left of him. One was a man with long, dirty blonde hair that fell at his shoulders and a shorter woman whose perfectly straight black hair framed her caring face.

The woman with colorful hair made her way towards him. "Who are you?"

He raised his eyebrows as the other two also came closer. "My name is Anon. I wanted to ask you all the same thing."

"I'm Zayika." Her voice was bold and strong.

"My name is Saige." the other woman told him. "And this is—"

"Zekiel." The man with hair covering his eyes reached out and shook his hand once they got close enough.

"Let's try to figure out where we are and get out of here." Zayika led the way.

Anon began walking with the three for a while. No one had a watch or cellphone to keep track of the time, but they collectively knew that several hours had passed by as the sun was eventually setting in a sky unlike anything they'd ever seen before. It wasn't the regular blue that they were used to, it was a green even brighter than the hills they woke up on. He tried to get to know the others as well as he could, but everyone was having difficulties about opening up or comprehending what was happening to them. It wasn't until Zayika spotted someone else running around off in the distance that their uncertainty grew even more.

"Look! There's a man over there!" she called out. "Why were we all brought here?"

"He's moving very quickly." Zekiel said. "Seems like he's also desperate to leave."

"Yeah, where is he going?" Saige seemed to have been holding her breath as she anxiously watched the stranger running for his life.

"This might be the man who brought me here. He was also moving very fast." Anon jumped in.

"Whoever this is, he seems scared out of his mind and trying to find help." Zayika furrowed her eyebrows. "I could be wrong, but it looks like he's leaving the hills and heading towards... a cliff? I don't see land past that point up ahead."

Anon felt a rush of concern as he noticed what she was referring to. There was some type of dead end in the hillside area that the man was heading straight for. It seemed unbeknownst to him that the road ended there from what the four could see.

Zayika looked away. "Well. He's totally going to fall off."

"We have to save him!" Anon responded.

"Go ahead and rescue him then, hero." she snickered.

Anon took her words seriously and began sprinting as quickly as he could back over the hills, up and down, tripping a few times on his shoelaces and frantically calling out after the stranger.

"I didn't think he would actually go after him." Zayika told Saige and Zekiel.

"Good on him for trying to save someone else." Saige responded as she looked over at her blonde haired companion. "We have to look out for each other here."

Her words inspired Zayika as she redirected her attention back to the two men. Anon lunged forwards and tackled him, both falling to the ground dangerously close to the planet's edge. The three ran over to witness what would take place next.

"What are you doing?" Anon asked him. "You need to relax, man, you were just about to have a really bad fall."

"I don't know where I am!" He was panicking.

"None of us do. We're trying to figure that out."

"Who are you?" with raised eyebrows he spoke hesitantly.

"I'm Anon. You?"

"Omar." he responded. "Thank you for saving me Anon. I owe you my life."

Zayika smiled.

The two got up, dusted themselves off, and Omar was officially introduced to Zayika, Saige, and Zekiel. The five wandered through the planet for a while and tried to scout out others who could inform them of where they had been taken. They heard yells and other noises coming from the jungle and ocean. When circling back towards the mounds of hills, they saw a figure in the distance who they'd never seen before. The night made it more difficult for them to check if the person was holding any weapons — or if they were a threat at all.

"I'm going to see who that is." Anon stated. "I'll go introduce myself."

"You're not going alone. We'll join you." Zayika informed him.

"That person is coming towards us." Omar said nervously as he stood behind everyone else.

"Let's meet halfway then." Anon seemed excited to meet someone new and led the way in front of the four that were following after him.

"Who are you?" he yelled out.

"I'm not here to hurt you! I'm lost and looking for safety." Amira replied with her hands in the air. "Can any of you help me?"

Present

After parting ways with Amira, I went towards Nathaniel's underground bunker to look for the Over Ground representative. There weren't many other places that she could hideaway without being out in the open since the planet ended at certain boundaries. *Why doesn't she send herself home? Is she really so loyal to the planet that she would choose to stay here and oversee each game for the rest of her life?* There must've been some type of irresistible incentive or invisible force keeping her at Eunoia. For some reason she was the one out of three representatives who put her arm in the air to take Amira and I back to Earth. *She holds so much power. The light she creates can literally make dreams come true.* It was clear that she had also been morphed in order to harness such an ability that was so important to the game we were in.

I tried to hold my head high as worry built up in me. *What if she doesn't have the answers to my questions? Can I live with myself never knowing the truth?* Uncertainty started to eat away at me as a feeling of despair turned into a pit in my stomach. My intuition was telling me that something was off, somewhere, but there was no sign of what truly was to come. I went down the rusted set of stairs and through the bunker's hallway to look around. I didn't see her in the first room and decided to use my voice to find her.

"Hello?" I spoke timidly.

There was no response. *I'm sure she's hiding.*

I continued, "You don't have to worry. This is Anon. I'm here to talk to you about the wishes."

The representative suddenly appeared from Nathaniel's old bedroom. "Where is Zayika?"

"I'm not sure right now. She's somewhere on the planet looking for me, actually. Do you mind if we speak for a little while? I have some questions to ask you."

"There was no option but to bring you back here. Zayika would've killed me if I didn't." she told me. "Are you here to fight me too?"

"It's not about that." I tried to alleviate her stress. "I believe what you're saying. I know what she is capable of and I'm sure she forced you to bring Amira and me back. There's other things I want to ask you about."

I stood before her with holes in my shirt, biting my lips in a helpless manner. She motioned for me to come into the room and sit on one of the unsteady supply crates.

She exhaled quickly. "I was so worried that you were her. She almost dropped me off of the cliff. I thought she was back to finish the job."

I realized that I still didn't know any of the representatives' names. "We never properly met, huh?" I reached out to shake her hand. "You know my name already, but what is yours?"

"Theia."

"It's nice to meet you. I'm sorry I didn't introduce myself in the past."

"The past is over. All that matters now is the present. Please don't worry about it." She leaned forward, elbows on her legs, and unexpectedly began crying into her palms.

Since I left the bunker door open I could hear leaves blowing around outside and an intense downpour of rain that was in sync with her own tears. A chill came over me. *The planet is crying too.*

"W-what's wrong?"

"All of this. Eunoia. It wasn't supposed to be this way." She wiped a tear and looked attentively at me. "When us three representatives made the waterfall portal… we never thought that our vision would end up in ruins and be the cause of so much destruction. Lorelai and Aadavan are gone now. I'm the only representative left. There should have been many more Wish Carriers back on Earth right now. The death count here is so high. This place was never meant to separate people, it was supposed to bring them together. Wishes were granted so that dreams could come true for those who proved to be mentally equipped to return to society."

"I don't understand something." I nervously ran my fingers through my wet hair.

"What?" Theia asked.

"Why would we be brought here to kill each other then? How is that enforcing a peaceful or 'beautiful' mindset? Why couldn't we have used our wishes without hurting one another?"

"The stakes needed to be high. Dying is part of life. There is a cycle of life that can't be changed on Earth and we wanted the same to be true for Eunoia. Death is promised to everybody."

I gulped loudly. "There's something else that I don't understand. Something that you didn't do that's... stuck in my mind."

"What did I not do?"

"At the end of the ceremony when you were there with Zayika, Amira, and me, you didn't correct me when I told Zayika that I couldn't wish for both of them to return. I was never told that I could have spared each. Why didn't you tell me?" I felt my heart rate rising with outrage. "In fact, why did Lorelai from the Oceanic Guardian faction even tell us what she did at the opening ceremony? We were lied to! At the beginning we were never told about Wish Carriers and many other things!"

Theia crossed her legs while sitting on the edge of the bunker's bed. "The rules that Lorelai announced at the opening ceremony weren't a complete lie, and there was a time when those were completely applicable. The planet created a stone and started to think for itself. In the jungle that piece of information appeared one day and Eunoia overrode our manifestation and original plans for the laws here. Aadavan used his ability to bring on a horrendous earthquake, hoping that the stone would be destroyed since we couldn't find another way to do so. Clearly we failed and your group still found out the planet's truth. We lost control of our vision and it began to control us."

"I still don't get why you did not correct me at the closing ceremony before you threw a burst of light in the air."

"It wasn't my place to. In the ceremony you were told that you could bring someone back to life, wish for immortality, in fact anything you've ever wanted. You saw Amira. When you told Zayika that you couldn't bring her back too, that was you subconsciously voicing what you wanted the rules to be."

"It just still doesn't make sen—"

"Let me ask you this, Anon." Theia sat upright. "When you all discovered the planet's stone and its engravings… do you recall it ever stating that a Wish Carrier could only bring one person with you?"

I thought back on the conversation with Amira at the waters before the earthquake happened. She revealed to me that she was also a Wish Carrier but never told me how only one person could be taken home.

"Amira wasn't from our faction, so I spared her life."

"You could have wished for anything, quite literally anything at all. You were designated as a Wish Carrier by the planet, so you technically had no boundaries or limitations."

"But you told us that members from different factions couldn't both go to Earth at the ceremony! You told us that right then! You—"

"We lied."

My mouth fell open in shock. I stood up abruptly and began pacing around the room. It felt like my entire world was crumbling. "Why? Why would you three do this?"

"Call it… denial?" Theia inhaled sharply. "It was hard to accept that the planet created its own set of rules. Us three were the masterminds behind the waterfall and its creation. We wanted to reset it and find a way to rework the rules to fit what our vision was aligned for."

I could have taken Zayika to Earth? Saved Omar and Saige's lives? Retrieved Zekiel from the darkness? Wished for time to be reversed and for all of the loss, heartache, and devastation to have never existed? "Are you joking?"

"You can't blame me entirely for your own oversights."

I let out a scream of heartbreak and threw a shard of lightning at the wall in front of me, narrowly missing Theia. "You are wrong for this!"

"What? Are you going to kill me?"

I tried to control my actions. *Jameson is here and has a wish. Don't kill Theia or else we will all be trapped forever. I need to talk to Jameson, Amira, and Zekiel. We can reverse everything and wish for our lives to be healed and restored.*

"No. I won't hurt you." I didn't want her to be scared of me. "I think our conversation is done here. I'm going to go outside and find the others."

"I hope you can understand where I'm coming from and the vision that the three of us manifested for this planet."

I will never understand any vision that a mind like hers would have.

I left the room we were in and went back through the hallway. While venturing up the bunker's stairs again, I tried to comprehend the news that was just delivered to me. *I can't believe this. I have to sacrifice my wings no matter how painful it is. I need to make everything right with Jameson's wish.* As I crept out from the bunker I almost fell backwards at the sight of Zayika standing before me. She was holding her head high, hair swaying back and forth wickedly in the wind as it always did.

"I found you." She put her hand towards me. "Need help maintaining your balance? You look like you're about to pass out."

"No. Just go away. This is not the time to torture me with more words." I tried to spring up and fly into the air, but she promptly knocked me down with a star current. All of the lightning scars on my skin throbbed at her heat and I tried to hide how much she was impairing me.

"You don't get to run away like you love doing. You will face your problems right here and now. Your time is not your own anymore."

"Please stop acting like I'm so selfish!" I shouted at her. "Please! Zayika, do you not remember me saving Omar on the hills at the beginning of this all? When he almost ran off the edge?"

"Whoa. You're mentioning that? You wouldn't have even noticed him if it wasn't for me bringing it up."

She's putting up a front. I could tell back in that moment that she noticed my actions and was moved by them.

"That doesn't matter. I saw him heading towards an early death and used all of my energy to go help."

Zayika shrugged her shoulders. "If focusing on that has helped you sleep at night, Anon, then I guess that's fine. But it doesn't make you a hero. Do you know how I can say that so confidently?"

"Just spit out your feelings once and for all. I'm sick of hearing them." My eyes met hers while I was hunched over near the ground.

"Because you made another tremendously idiotic decision by coming here by yourself." She was on the verge of laughing.

"What are you talking about?"

"Seriously? Are you that stupid? I know what's going on. Did you really think that I haven't been observing the rest of you this entire time when I've gotten the chance?"

I bit into my lip. "What have you heard?"

"I know that Jameson is a Wish Carrier and you all want to get back to Earth."

"How does working with them make me stupid?"

She got down on her knees in front of me and put a hand on my shoulder. "Anon, why did you not bring the other three with you to find the representative? You knew that Jameson had a wish... and that she could grant wishes. But you, yet again, were only focused on your feelings and selfish thoughts. Now I've been given even more power, which I didn't think was possible. I'm assuming that you three were working with the new guy, right? I would've had to get rid of him in order to stop your plan but it looks like you ended up ruining it all on your own. Nice job. You have somehow managed to fall below the already very low expectations that I had for you."

Damn it. I felt my heartbeat rising in my chest and became lightheaded. *Wait, I didn't... she is right.*

"But I—"

"No more excuses. You deserve the fate you've brought upon yourself." She kicked dirt in my face and stood up.

This can't be happening!

"I have hardly gotten any sleep since I left Eunoia because you haunt my dreams!"

She was taken aback by my words. "What was I saying, or doing, in them?"

"You were repeating the words you said to me when we left you, over and over again. Some nights you would speak the same ones to me that you did when I was in a trance after Omar died."

"I asked you what words I said. Tell me exactly what they were."

My heart was about to beat out of my chest. "You promised that you would make me regret what I did and how you would never forget me."

Right as I finished my sentence, the storm fully overtook the planet's sky. Everything was overshadowed with vibrant hues of purple and pink, similarly to the blue trance. Rain poured relentlessly and thunder reverberated above us. A solid blue bolt of lightning shot down nearby and left two small craters in the ground.

Zayika's green eyes shone brightly at the ray of brightness it brought. "It looks like this is a sign, Anon. My words were true… I never did and never will forget you. It's finally time for me to fulfill my promise. No more gimmicks or wasted time."

CHAPTER ELEVEN: CONSEQUENCES

Zayika

Present

Everything I waited for was finally within my reach. I managed to bring Anon and Amira back to Eunoia for getting the revenge I needed so desperately. They tried to run and hide, but the times I would let them run off and talk to each other never lasted long. There was a slim chance that I'd be outsmarted by the others. *Theia knows better than to grant Jameson's wish without me present. She knows that I would get rid of her like Lorelai and Aadavan if she got in my way.* I wanted to draw out the chase against me to make their skin crawl. *They deserve to feel helpless, abandoned, and let down. They deserve to feel as awful as I did.*

I found Anon exiting the bunker. His negligence was absolutely outstanding. *How is he so blind to opportunity? It's almost as if he doesn't want to see it.* I'd never met someone who thought as awfully under pressure as he did. I enjoyed embarrassing him, but he did a great job of doing that on his own. Somehow he didn't piece together how important it was to bring Jameson with him to find the representative. *Anon's going to try to appeal to my emotions, but he'll realize soon enough that nothing he can say or do will make me care. His feelings don't matter. I will not be manipulated.*

"Amira and I regret what we chose!" he tried to plead with me. "I feel awful about what I did, Zayika!"

"Good." I gave a genuine smile. *You should feel that way.*

I wasn't going to be walked on like a doormat by people with dirty shoes. Eunoia was advocating for me to win. The planet gave me unimaginable powers that allowed me to do almost anything I wanted. *No one else was as strong as me after being morphed. Betrayal was meant to happen. Being left behind has made me even stronger than the stars that I command.* From the start I already knew that making friends would be a waste of time, so I never allowed myself to get attached. But having someone owe me a favor? Them feeling as though they owe me their life? I couldn't get that type of thrill out of my head. Being the one in power was always my calling. The planet chose me to be the one to deal out the justice that others were too weak to do.

Fools like Anon didn't contribute to society. He was as selfish as anyone could be, so it was fitting that he and Amira naturally fell in love. Her selfishness was also glaringly evident at the closing ceremony. Both of them were a perfect match. *Sure I might be consumed with revenge, but at least I care about others getting what they deserve. I care about something that surpasses myself.* Anon wasn't a real friend to those he pretended to be invested in. He didn't use his extraordinary wish to revive Omar at the castle ruins, save doe-eyed Saige from the sharpened knife, or ask for Zekiel to be spit out of the planet's mysterious vacuum. *It's obnoxiously bold for someone to claim that they want to lead others... but not care for their wellbeing.* None of us were even in the back of his very small and dusty mind besides the woman he wanted to impress.

I was always more suited to be the leader of us all. Anon would have been put into his place much sooner. The game on Eunoia was never meant to be us thirty competing for a ticket to Earth, it truly began once Amira and Anon fell back into the misty ocean. When I stumbled upon my white dress before having them brought back I realized something invaluable… *Who says I can't be the leader? I don't need to have followers here. I am my own leader and follower.* Nero or Jameson didn't team up with me, I didn't need them, but having their assistance could've been useful at times. Regardless of who helped me, I refrained from becoming invested. Putting emotion and time into others never went well. I was eventually stabbed in the back by them and had to clean up my own blood along with their blade while they tried to salt my wounds. There was only myself to look out for and satisfy. What would please me the most? Concluding everything. *Time for justice.* Our time was up and there could be no more chasing. The only task still remaining was to deal out the consequences that were due.

I grabbed Anon by his shoulders viciously, digging my fingernails into his already bruised skin after I discovered him leaving Nathaniel's dirty hideout. It was time to bring him to the ocean. As Nero arrived at the same location as us two, I shot him a puzzled look that I followed with an enticing smile. He looked at my hand that was on Anon and seemed just as perplexed.

"Where have you been?" I asked him. "Did you not find the Over Ground representative? I could've used your help back there."

"No, I didn't find her. I got lost in that insanely tall wheat field. This was the last place I was going to check." Nero responded.

"Well she's not past that concrete door." Anon stated.

"That sucks." Nero said to him and then refocused his attention on me. "It looks like you've got Anon where you want him."

"We're not there yet. Maybe your statement will be truer when he's six feet under."

He walked over and whispered in my ear, "I get what it's like to be passionate, but don't you think you're directing your attention on the wrong thing?"

I whispered back out of Anon's range of hearing, "I know what I'm doing. If you want to focus on getting back to Earth, then you can do that. I don't care about my old world anymore. I want peace of mind. Closure."

Nero's dark eyes showed concern. "Are you sure? You don't have to hurt yourself in the process of trying to hurt him. Let's find the representative together and get back to where we should be."

I huffed. "Your words don't incentivize me at all to follow your desires. I know what I'm doing."

"What are you both talking about?" Anon interrupted.

I stepped away from Nero and refocused my attention on him, "Oh yeah… I forgot that you always have to have everyone's attention. We were just talking about who is going to hit you first."

Anon was scared as he went back and forth between observing Nero and me. "I want to get back to Amira."

"Why did you part from her in the first place?" I asked him. "Why do you constantly make such bad decisions? You know what? Let's head to my favorite part of the planet—the ocean. Your journey will end at the same place you ruined the start of it at."

"I thanked you for saving my life!" Anon retorted with a whiny voice.

"Actions will always say more than words do."

I created an orb of spinning white, purple, and yellow stars and blindsided Anon with rope-like structures that sprang from it. They started to tie his wrists together and I pinned him down helplessly. *Just how I like things.*

"Get these off!" he demanded. "Seriously, why are you doing this?"

"Because using force is required in order to get you where you need to be."

Anon attempted to activate the lightning in his arms and hands to break down my restraints, but it didn't work out how he wanted. All he did was zap himself repeatedly and became more frustrated at me and his own self for inflicting pain. Sparks were flying and he winced at each one.

"So… anyways… I'm going to head out. This kind of stuff really isn't for me." Nero said.

"I don't think so." I recreated the orb again and tried to entangle him as he turned away.

"No!" Nero yelled.

He quickly shot out a gust of wind that knocked me backwards. My own stars were dimmed by him and I bit into the side of my mouth deeply in the process. *He's not stupid, so why is he turning against me?*

"You don't want to be on the wrong side of history, Nero." I bounced back up and dusted off my boots. "Don't cross me like this. Why not be my ally on the beach? I promise that it will be fun."

"I told you no." He furrowed his eyebrows. "I am on my own side, no one else's, and I don't answer to others.

You aren't going to pull me around on a leash too. I am not your bitch."

"Oh stop being so touchy! Just go along with things like Anon over there." I gave a snarky wave which made him shake his head with contempt. "Relax. Your time's coming soon."

Nero faked a loaded grin. "You seem to not know me too well, Zayika, if you think I operate the same way that he does."

"Alright then." I looked over my dress, making sure there were no scuff marks on it from my fall. "Prove me wrong. Actually try to fight me. If you can get a really good hit in, then I'll let you decide where you go at your own leisure."

"What have I done to have become a target to you?"

"Curiosity."

"What if I refuse?" Nero's already deep voice became rough like gravel when he felt challenged.

"Then I eliminate you, which shouldn't be that hard to do."

"If you're going to stand in my way then I have no other choice." He wasted no time pulling a serrated throwing knife out of his pocket. "I'll defend myself."

"Awesome." I crafted stars again and leapt into the air, carrying myself closer to him.

Wind gushed out of Nero's left hand as the other was occupied with his weapon of choice. *Try to burn him just like Aadavan.* I took a deep breath and channeled my ability again. *Heal myself if I need to.* It was surprising how strong the currents that he created were, they caused me to momentarily lose my balance and interrupted my train of thought. I shot out a ray of piping hot stars at him and he narrowly dodged the attack by swiftly leaning into a full body roll in the opposite direction. *He's always also been quick on his feet.* When I went to breathe in again, it was as if the air was taken out of my lungs. My eyes widened at the sight of Nero hovering above the ground while simultaneously using it to strangle me.

"As I said—I will defend myself." He tightened his hold. "I wasn't joking about that."

My hands frantically met my throat as I shook my head. My power was slowly draining away as my need for air rapidly increased. He took that window of time to make use of the blade resting in his fingertips and aimed it for my face. My dodge wasn't fast enough as he utilized wind currents alongside the knife to expedite its journey. One of my ears was cleanly sliced off and fell next to Anon. Nero let go of his grip on me and steadily returned to the dirt below. Blood was seeping out of me, so I hastily healed myself. My left ear reattached and I abruptly let my lungs refill again to take a deep breath.

"Shall we keep going?" he asked.

I put a hand up at him and then placed it onto my chest. "Forget it. I'm not going to use any more energy that I could be saving for Anon and Amira on you."

"I really don't mind." Anon chimed in shakily from the sidelines.

"Shut up. You have no say in anything." I told him in between breaths.

"So are you going to stay out of my way? I have the right to make my own decisions." Nero shoved his hand into his back pocket.

"Whatever." I needed to stay on track.

"Great." He walked over towards Anon. "Let's go to the ocean then."

"You're coming with us?" I asked. "I thought you wanted to go separate ways."

"Don't be mistaken. I'm heading in the same direction as you both, as I have a plan of my own, but I want nothing to do with the vengeance you're seeking and won't assist in fulfilling your fantasies. I'm only going to see if the Over Ground representative made her way over there in the last hour or so."

Anon said nothing. *Of course this loser won't tell Nero if she is actually down in the bunker.*

"Fine." *There's no use in fighting Nero.*

I led Anon to the largest part of Eunoia's terrain with Nero trailing behind us. I was curious to see if his eyes would be opened and if he'd join in the blissful chaos that I was going to create. *Is he really that different from me?* I wasn't sure what to say to either of them after what happened and lightly touched my ear to make sure it was still there. *What a close call.*

"I have a question for you, Zayika." Anon broke the silence.

"What?" *He can try to apologize again, but it will mean nothing to me.* "What is it now? If you're asking for us to seek out Amira, that's not going to happen. If she and that fish decide to make an oceanside appearance, then you can see her."

"What happened to you before you were brought to Eunoia? What is your story?"

"That doesn't matter." I said coldly while trying to suppress memories of my past.

"Of course it does. I thought it didn't either, but Omar sort of showed me that it does."

"You and Omar shared a heart-to-heart before he died? I'm not surprised. You two are the type to not shut up about your feelings."

"That's a bold statement Zayika, since you are fueled purely by vindictive feelings yourself." he shot back at me.

"Wow. Can you both stop fighting for like two minutes?" Nero said. "You're going to make me take a different pathway."

"Literally no one asked to hear from you either." I told him. "You're no better than the two of us."

"You don't know me." Nero shot me a guarded look.

"Anon, it's none of your business what happened to me before all of this." I changed the topic. "But I'm sure you'd love to talk about yourself right now."

Anon breathed deeply. "I came from a broken household. My parents divorced and… they fought a lot."

I remained silent so he would continue taking my bait. *Is he serious?* Nero didn't speak either.

"I won't get into the details about how bad things got, but I tried to be a mediator. I attempted to fix things. I'll be honest, though, deep down I've always felt that I am the reason their relationship fell apart. I was never supposed to be born. I try to solve problems, but I make them worse when I do, so I…"

"Run away." I finished his sentence. "You storm out."

The stormy weather complemented our conversation. Thunder bellowed in the sky as Anon looked directly at me. "Why do you think I am so excited to have found Amira? Someone that I believe will remain a part of my life in the long run? Why do you think I try so hard to lead others in a positive direction?"

I refrained from rolling my eyes. "I'm not unobservant, Anon. I know that you're only telling me your life story so that I can have a change of heart to spare you and forgive how you've wronged me."

His eyes lit up and Nero looked skeptical.

"But I'm not that type of person." I completed my sentiment. "Anon, it's people like you that deserve consequences. Others can save your life, risk their own for yours, but you don't care. You only care about your selfish desires, and nothing can get in your way of achieving them."

Nero spoke up again before Anon could respond, "We've made it to the ocean."

Four Months Before

It was the week before Andrea's birthday party. Everyone went to a restaurant and caught up on stories when Myles abruptly left the table and stormed out of an exit. Zayika noticed this and saw how his stiff and tense posture was brought on by a mysterious figure passing by one of the windows outside. No one else seemed to question or care about what was happening with him, but she couldn't stop wondering what he was doing in the alleyway with someone she'd never seen before. Zayika grew curious with each passing minute and decided to excuse herself to check on the situation. She stepped out into the chilling air, secured her dark brown hair into a loose ponytail, and pulled her jacket tightly around herself.

"Is everything alright?" Her voice was smooth and broke the obvious tension.

"Go back inside. This is none of your business." Myles told her.

"Give me what I asked for or else I hit the send button." the stranger said to her friend with his phone screen held high. "Your girlfriend will know the truth."

"Myles, do you want me to get Allison?" Zayika asked.

"No!" he shouted at her. "Just go back to the table! I'll be in soon!"

The other man tapped the checkmark on his smartphone screen, which made Myles to spring into a panicked state. Out of nowhere he pulled out a large knife and shoved it into his stomach.

"What are you doing?" Zayika was in shock. "What are you doing to him?"

Myles didn't answer but instead repeatedly jammed the knife into him over and over again next to the restaurant's trash cans.

"You brought this on yourself." he was told as the stranger died at his hands.

Zayika turned to go back to the others, but Myles sprinted and got a hold of her arm to whisper in her ear. "I will make sure your life is destroyed if you tell anyone about this."

He put the bloody knife down into the pocket of her black jacket.

"Why are you giving this to me?"

"Because I need you to get rid of it. Don't speak a word about what you saw or else you'll be sorry. If you so much as give me the wrong look or act like you're going to rat me out, I promise you will regret it."

"Don't worry…" Zayika responded quietly. "I would also kill someone if I needed to."

She was surprised at her words, almost as if she wasn't the one who said them. *Where did that come from?* She was unsure but felt a surge of frustration at Myles' recklessness with her being caught in the middle. She was in disbelief at the thought of him getting away with his actions… and also filled with envy.

Present

Anon watched the waves up ahead in terror next to me. I could see he sensed that the worst was about to come. *I'm not going to be invisible, not say what's on my mind, and will never be a coward. I will destroy who I have to. This itch has to be scratched.* I released him from my handcuffs of stars and stretched my arms up into the air. It was so entertaining seeing the fear in his eyes every time he looked at me, not able to fake even an ounce of power.

"So what should I do?" I asked myself out loud.

Nero was still confused. "What really is the point of this, Zayika?"

I ignored his question and in the blink of an eye swung stars to slit Anon's throat in a singular sharp movement. Blood was bursting out of his neck as he desperately tried placing his hands over the fatal wound.

Nero was disturbed. "What the—"

"You aren't going to die yet, Anon, don't worry!"

Anon tried to talk but instead choked on the blood in his throat. "Plea-se help m—"

"Come on, Zayika, I think this is enough." Nero interrupted.

I let out a laugh as I started to pull stars downwards, soft and glistening with comfort as they surrounded Anon and began healing him. I smiled, not because I saved his life again, but because I knew what to do next. Each of my fingers had different dark fantasies assigned to them. It was time to start pointing them around with the intent to bring each to life. *Pace this out correctly. He can't go yet. He has to suffer.*

"I'm so sorry for what I did to you, okay?" Anon sprinted towards me as his wispy black hair fell over his eyes, pleading for forgiveness. "Give me another chance!" His neck was fully healed.

"Why would I?" *Fool.* "You didn't even give me one to begin with. This is what happens when you make the wrong decision." I looked over at Nero with hungry eyes, "Your turn."

"No." He backed away. "I just want to get to Earth, not torture someone."

I used my stars to pull one of Nero's knives out of his pocket and twisted around to face Anon in a split second. This time I shoved the knife directly into his right eye before he could block the attack. A searing pain overcame his entire being as he promptly fell down in agony and held onto his face. The fun wasn't over yet. *Where is Amira? She should be watching this.*

"Stop! Stop! Stop!" Tears were flowing out from Anon's other eye.

"What's the matter Anon? Can you only remember one word right now?" I crouched over him. "What does that feel like? Does it feel as though you're losing your mind? It's not pleasant, is it?"

Nero walked up beside me. "Zayika, if you don't stop this, I will step in."

I shook my head. "If you don't want to join then just leave. Why do you even care at all? You aren't perfect either if you stand by and choose to watch this." I reached my arm out and grabbed onto the side of Anon's neck and noticed that his skin wasn't changing. "Why are you not using your lightning against me? Did your batteries run out? What type is it that you run on?"

"Stop!" He yanked himself away from me and rolled on the rocky ground, cuts and bruises littering his skin as he flailed and accidentally shoved the knife further into his eye socket. His yelps echoed in the air as thunder struck in the distance. A ray of lightning crashed down over the sea, outlining his body.

"Might be time to heal again unless you're done with him." Nero went to retrieve the blade out of his face.

"Ugh fine." I took a deep breath and commanded my stars to heal Anon once again.

"How many times can you do that before it runs out?" Nero asked. "What happens if it stops working?"

"Then he dies." I blurted out with enjoyment. "I'd not like that to be so soon, but it's also not the worst outcome."

Nero noticed a figure watching us from the distance and a chill washed over me when I saw it too. *Who is that?* They stood perfectly still, making no sound or movement as they watched on, like they were in disbelief at what was taking place. "Someone is observing us." Nero said. It looked like there were two other people behind them. *Is that Jameson? Amira? They seem to be the right height, but who are they with? I can't let my guard down.*

"Whatever! I love audiences." I went back over to Anon again, only letting myself be distracted for just a moment. This time I aimed for his spine and created my own blade of stars to dig deep into his back near his wings. Anon laid lifelessly on the ground, barely speaking. "Get up and fight back!" I shouted at him.

"I-I can't move my legs!" his strained voice yelped.

"I think I paralyzed him!" I spun in a celebratory manner until coming to a staggering halt once I noticed Nero still staring at the others with a tightened fist. "What's going on?" *Since when does Nero get worried about anything?*

Four Months Before

Zayika raced over to a side door of the house with a bloody knife behind her back. Andrea was close by and kept her mouth closed, fearful and confused about what was going to come next. It took several knocks for them to get an answer. The rain poured heavily as they waited and didn't speak to each other. One of their friends eventually greeted them with a hint of annoyance.

"Zayika, what are you both doing here?" he asked.

"You know why I'm here." Zayika responded. "Let us in so we can talk."

"I'm sort of busy right no—"

"I don't care, Myles. I think you know what's at stake if you don't let me in, so I advise that you cooperate before things escalate." Her silver and purple hair was soaking wet as she bounced her head up and down with each syllable of her calculated words.

"Ugh. Fine."

Myles let the two women inside the garage of his parents' house as they greeted the others who were sitting around talking.

"You didn't come to the party so that you could have one of your own?" Zayika spoke louder than everyone else. "Really?"

"We're sorry. We didn't find out until the last second about your birthday Andrea." one of the women said from the corner.

Zayika gave her a kind smile and then shot a hateful glare at Myles. "Why is that? Why did you not do what you were supposed to and show up?"

"Just let it go." Myles told her. "I'm not sure if anyone has told you this, but you need to learn how to let things go. Stop making a scene."

"Do you want them to know the truth?" Zayika asked in a livid tone.

"Forget this. Get out of here. You hold no power over me." He tried to usher her and Andrea back through the door, but Zayika planted her sopping boots firmly on the ground.

"You see this?" She held up the knife that she had been concealing. "It's time you all found out the truth about your friend—the one you blindly follow and worship. This weapon is Myles'... and he killed someone with it."

Myles knocked it out of her hands and shoved Zayika to the ground. "How dare you talk about this! What about our deal?"

"What 'deal'? You blackmailing me after I saw you stab someone to death? Forget it! Go ahead and destroy my career that I've worked so hard for, I don't even care anymore!" Zayika looked around the room at everyone nervously watching them. "I will not let you hold power over me! I hold it over you!"

"You annoying bitch. You're really that jealous? No one here thinks you are important. You're going to misconstrue what you saw in order to make me sound like the bad one?"

"I know what I saw." Her voice was full of certainty. "Myles, you aren't who you claim to be."

"What will you do about your ridiculous lie? Report me? Tell the cops?" Myles looked at his other friends. "Let's say what she's saying is true, would you all rat me out?"

His loyal followers shook their heads in disagreement.

"How pathetic." Zayika slowly stood up. "Actions should have consequences. Screw your cult."

"Who's to say that you aren't the one who committed murder with that weapon? After all, why do you have it then?"

"You can't twist this against me!"

"You admitted to me that you'd be okay killing a person if you'd needed to. You're only making this look worse for yourself. Go home. I can't promise that you'll have a job or future at all thanks to the rift you've caused. I should have never associated myself with you." Miles spit on the ground in front of her.

She glanced at everyone with a defeated look. Skeptical stares and judgmental expressions were all that surrounded her. "Karma will come for you." her voice shook.

Irritation was festering in Zayika's mind at what took place that night. She couldn't stop thinking about his actions as several mornings, evenings, and nights passed. Eventually the words he spoke to her was all that she could hear, even when others were actually trying to catch her attention. She thought to herself, *Karma is taking too long*. On a lonely summer morning she got into her car and went back to his house with determination to seek vengeance.

She lured him over to her vehicle, which was stopped at the side of the road. "Just talk to me for a few minutes."

"Why?" Myles groaned and leaned over the open window. "What is it that you want? What makes you think I want to talk to you?"

"I'm the one who needs to say something."

He sighed while moving into the passenger side and closed the door. "Alright, fine, what do you ne —"

Zayika hurriedly leapt over and forced him backwards by pulling the lever at his feet and pushing back the seat with her other hand. In a split second she took the seat belt next to him and yanked it up against his neck. Myles started to suffocate and was unable to speak as he looked at her with regret.

"Oh come on. What did you think was going to happen?" She was on the verge of laughing. "I had to get the job done myself since karma was taking forever to catch up to you."

Present

"It's him again." Nero pointed to the unknown person looking at us and muttered something under his breath.

"Who are you? Come out now!" I lit up my stars to force them to come into view like I had done in the ocean.

We all kept our words to ourselves once my question was answered. Zekiel was approaching us with Jameson and Amira beside him. *Jameson should be smart enough to not use his wish to save them.* Thunder rang out again. *I'll make sure that doesn't happen if he tries.*

"Zekiel?" I felt uncomfortable for some reason when I saw his face. His eyes were emotionless and the whites of them seemed as though they had melted away. "You're alive?"

He shook his head at us. "I'm dead." He remained still and spoke heavily from his chest.

"What are you talking about?" Jameson asked, like he'd never seen the broken part of Zekiel, even though he was right next to him.

"You left the void alongside Nero." It all made sense to me. "So you've been out for a little while. I see you met the newcomer and… also found Amira."

"Amira! Please help me!" Anon interjected. "I can't walk! I need your help!"

I shoved Anon's head down forcefully, his nose taking the most impact. "Shut up. Either you help your own self or you die here."

"Leave him alone!" Amira began storming over with brave footsteps and I put a hand up in her direction, causing her to momentarily stop. "I will call for Hippo." She tried to threaten me.

I'm not sure how long I can keep that mutated fish away. I can stun it like last time, but that doesn't hold for long. Whatever. I'll figure it out. Hippo can't defeat me, she'll only make this fight more amusing.

Zekiel spoke while staring off into nothingness, not making eye contact with anyone. "I wish I didn't make it back. Suffering is all I can feel. I need to get back to the void. Take me back. I can't handle being this... aware."

"Aware of what?" I asked. *He sounds like a madman.*

"Of losing Jasmine, Saige, and... myself." He started shaking as he got closer. "Take me back through the portal, please." He looked down at Anon. "Is the game still going on?"

"No Zekiel, it's not. Are you being serious? Get a clue." I chuckled. "The game ended a long time ago. We haven't seen each other in a while, huh? Well since Amira and Jameson somehow failed to catch you up, I will. It's simple—Anon betrayed me, so now he's paying for that mistake."

"Let me tear out both of his wings. I can take him away and escape too." Zekiel said with a straight face, as he usually did.

I'd be lying if I said I'm not tempted by his offer, but I don't want Anon to get off that easily. Is Zekiel putting up a front right now? His words seem... rehearsed.

"You going too wasn't part of the pl—" Jameson was interrupted by being roughly nudged by Zekiel. "Never mind." He then whispered something along the lines of creating a diversion.

"Don't tell me that you're working for them, Jameson." I gave him a mischievous half-smile.

My attention wasn't focused much on Jameson and Zekiel since I cared more about fulfilling my destiny on Eunoia. Amira held her head high in a stance that told me everything I needed to know. *She's not the type to back down and never has been.* I healed Anon, who was still stuck on the ground and unable to walk, to let him get back on his feet. He immediately turned to face Amira.

"Hey." His eyes warmed as they focused on hers. "How are you doing?"

"I should be asking you that." She helped him stand up. "Where have you been? What did you do? I wish you would've taken me with you."

"He should have but understanding why he needed to was apparently too much critical thinking for him." I jumped in.

"What is she talking about?" Amira gently placed her hand on his neck.

"I think I really messed up." he held back tears as his voice cracked. "Amira, I'm really sorry. You deserve better than this."

"Just tell me what happened. I will forgive you."

The planet's storm was getting impatient, just like I was. The trance couldn't wait any longer. Wind blew through my hair and a multitude of upside-down clouds above us reflected in the waves, their milky-white eyes were watching me.

"W-why does the sky look like that?" Jameson stammered.

"Eunoia is spectating." I blew a kiss at the clouds. "Don't worry, I'll make you proud for picking me."

"Zayika, what are you about to do?" Amira noticed how determined I had become.

"You're about to find out. All I will say is… you can thank Anon for what happens next." I walked towards the ocean with one of my arms out and used my stars to pull something out of it. "It's ironic how you both are the same height but can't see eye to eye."

"What are you doing?" Amira asked as her arm intertwined with Anon's.

I could tell that she was about to call Hippo over again, so I sped up my scheme. "I'm getting a gift for you. When you see it, you'll be well aware of what it is. It's your own personal consequence for being guilty by association, an accessory to the recklessness of Anon's asinine actions."

"Stop, please, stop running your mouth and—" She stopped speaking once she saw one of Hippo's wet broken teeth floating in the air like a feather in the wind.

I rested a small portion of the tooth onto my hand, using my abilities to sustain the size and weight of it above me. "Do you recognize this, Amira? Can you guess what it is?"

"You kept track of that when Hippo attacked the Land Dwellers?" She was beside herself. "Why would you?" She whispered for her fish to come out of the waters and I watched as it slowly arose nearby.

I don't care that her companion is here. She's easy to get rid of. "Because I thought, what if it could grant me special powers? Not like mine aren't enough already, but it still could have been nice." My green eyes demanded her to back down.

"What do you plan on doing with it?" Anon asked me uneasily.

"I'm going to do what I've dreamt about doing every single day and night since the two of you worthless beings left me for dead!" I shrieked and ran at Amira.

She put her hand out to motion for me to stop. *What you want means nothing to me. Absolutely nothing. Your feelings are not my concern, just as mine weren't to you.* Anon tried to start charging his lightning, but he couldn't concentrate enough to stop me. With all of my energy, I drove the very tip of Hippo's tooth roughly through Amira's chest. She stared at me in absolute shock. *Goodbye, Amira.* My fingers twitched as I let go and with a loud thud, it hit the ground as she put her hands up to her heart.

"W-what have you done?" she asked before falling to the ground.

"What I should have done when you first got here."

"No, no, no!" Anon screamed louder than ever before. He rushed to Amira's side and grabbed onto her tightly as tears flooded his eyes. "Amira, no, Amira!"

"How does it feel, Anon?" I asked him in a fit of rage.

"Why would you do this? I never took away someone you loved!"

"You might as well say goodbye soon, she's about to bleed out."

"Heal her! Come on!" Anon was begging. "Zayika! Don't do this! Why do you have to take everything so far?"

It felt good to see them broken. Anon was so helpless as Amira's journey abruptly came to an end. *Bet you never thought that a part of your companion would assist me in ending you. It doesn't feel right, does it? Neither was being stabbed by those who are beneath me. I'm untouchable now. Forever out of your reach.*

"Anon. I—" Amira laid her head on his chest as he stroked her hair. "I will miss you."

He tried to stop crying so that he could speak. "No! Not you... not like this. Amira. I'm not losing you. We will see each other again."

For the first time ever, I saw her cry.

"How do you know?" she asked.

"I just do. You're the person I was supposed to find."

"I enjoyed our time together. Despite what has been said, I think you've tried your best to do what's right... I love you, Anon."

"I love you too."

He leaned down and the two kissed each other softly. Anon watched on with a broken heart as life left Amira's eyes, his hands were covered in her blood. He pushed her eyelids closed and planted another shaky kiss on her forehead. The sight of them instantly reminded me of him being held by her after almost drowning in the ocean. *Was it worth it, Anon? You never should have tried to find that lighthouse. You should have never left me to die.* There was nothing but silence for a while. My heart raced as I noticed how Amira's blood was freshly splattered on my clothes. Jameson started pacing around and Zekiel looked like another small piece of him had been shattered. *Get a grip, you guys, like either of you really cared about her.* Nero let out a very deep sigh.

Anon was full of sorrow. "You were the best part of my life, Amira, the most beautiful part. You were the only good that came from this planet. You were the start of it all. Hope wasn't here until you arrived."

Nero looked at me like I took something too far and it irked me to my core.

"What Nero?" I broke my silence and shouted while stepping over Hippo's bloody tooth. "Are you really going to judge me? You of all people? The man here who has no morals?"

"That's not true! I do." he replied weakly as Anon wept next to us. "This is not what I want to be a part of. I don't like this, Zayika."

"Give me a break!" For some reason I felt like I was holding back tears of my own... and a grin from ear to ear. "You've been playing along this entire time! You killed Saige and couldn't care less! Plus, you've said it yourself that you think we are alike!"

"You were the one who made that assumption. I am not like you." he responded defensively.

"Whatever. You didn't deny it, so who's to say that some part of you isn't on my side?"

"I know that we are not the same after what you've just done." Nero shook his head. "You've made everything... different."

"Don't act like some sort of champion. It's too late to redeem yourself now." I was speaking to everyone on the shore, not just him. "It's time to kill you too, Anon. Let me ask you this... are you even going to fight back?"

Anon lovingly placed Amira on the ground while staring scornfully at me. "Of course I will."

CHAPTER TWELVE: SCARS

Nero

Present

It was extremely difficult to not pay attention to the train wreck that was before me. After exiting the void, I came across Zayika and learned about the conflict she was creating. *I have to stand my ground. Their issues have nothing to do with me.* I tried to remain concentrated on my goal of returning to Earth, but I was becoming increasingly frustrated at how cornered I was. Anon and the woman named Amira didn't have wishes to use anymore and Zayika never received one. *How am I going to get home?* The representative was nowhere to be found. I searched every deserted faction trying to discover where she was hiding. She wasn't in Nathaniel's bunker… at least that's what Anon said after searching it. *Why did I even believe him? He could've been lying! I shouldn't have gotten so distracted by him and Zayika.*

When I finally reached the ocean after defending myself against her, my intuition told me to go back to the bunker and see for myself if Anon wasn't telling me the truth. *I'm sure he lied. Why would he do anything to benefit me? We've never gotten along.* I mentally kicked myself for being naive at that moment. *I have to keep my head in the game.*

The Over Ground representative wasn't at the ocean either when we arrived. Everything escalated between the others when I quietly decided to go back to the bunker. Zayika was putting Anon through hell and tortured him over and over again. *I have to look away.* It was hard to fathom how much she sadistically enjoyed her actions. We all were at the shore when everything came full circle. Jameson and Amira showed up again with... Zekiel. *I have to agree to disagree with him, we will never see eye to eye, and maybe that is a good thing.* I kept myself from interfering with everyone else and tried to dodge their issues. For some reason they all seemed to be focused on anything other than getting to Earth, aside from Jameson, who I never got to know. *If he's an ally to Zekiel then I'm sure he isn't someone I want to get close to.*

It felt as though time was sped up on the planet with how fast everything was going sideways. After Anon was repeatedly tormented, Amira was killed by Zayika who impaled her through the chest with an enormous anglerfish tooth. Witnessing someone get murdered made me think of the lives I took at the Land Dweller faction. The sight of spewing blood and sounds of others saying what they know will be their last words reawakened a harsh feeling inside of me. *I want nothing to do with this.* I never cared for Anon, but watching him hold Amira as she died limply in his arms made me not think about his insufferable personality or how he irritated me anymore. *This isn't right. I need to get out of here. I have to search every inch of that bunker and convince my faction leader to let me go home. This isn't a game anymore.*

Zayika and Anon became consumed with trying to destroy each other. She wanted to bring out the worst in him, and he was about to fight that side of her. Neither cared about Earth anymore. Anon was a mess on the ground as Zekiel joined in the mayhem with an anguished spirit. *What if Anon's wings get taken off while he's getting attacked? I need to stay away from that portal if it opens again.* I didn't want anything to do with returning back to that meaningless void. I was entirely ready to go back to where I belonged, which was the only goal I kept track of since meeting Gebu and the rest of my faction. Zekiel started whispering something in Zayika's ear and for some reason Jameson was observing the two with a baffled look.

What is going on?

Zayika chuckled. "That's admirable, Zekiel, really. I like the thought of watching you two fight, but I sort of wanted to save Anon's demise for me. You understand what I'm saying... right? I mean if you were presented with the chance to kill the person who ruined your life you would, wouldn't you?"

It was as if a specific person came to Zekiel's mind when she said those words. I saw a split second of his tormented personality, even though his eyes were vacant. "You know nothing about me or my past, Zayika."

"Well if what I said was wrong, why did you get upset?" She played with others' emotions like they were puppets.

"Wait, what were you telling her?" Jameson tried to redirect Zekiel's attention over to him. "We need to regroup."

Seems like these two heroes aren't exactly on the same page.

The ocean started to rumble as a bright light shone out from its surface. "Is this some type of earthquake? Well, eunoiaquake?" I looked over at Zayika, who was livid.

"Since when do you make ridiculous jokes? No, unfortunately it's something much worse." she said sharply as a bright bulb started to appear. "She's back again."

A monster forcefully breached the waves with a giant orb lighting the way. I'd never seen a creature from Eunoia's sea before, let alone fought someone from the Oceanic Guardian faction. I remembered seeing a dazzling light from time to time in the ocean's deep trenches through my bedroom window before the fight of thirty began.

"Is this real?" I was in shock as I followed after Zayika.

"Obviously. Many mutation variations are possible here, Nero, we are living testimonies to that." She started to fill her palms up with luminous stars again. "This fish is named Hippo. It's Amira's companion."

I smacked my hands together. "Wow. That's actually quite awesome! There was a man in our faction with pet clouds that followed him around. Did you ever get the chance to meet him? His name was Varid."

Zayika spun around at me, her colorful hair tousled from the wind and sticking out in different directions. "What makes you think I care at all about that? Have you lost your mind?"

I hid a smirk as I answered, "Not the way that you have."

She glared.

I continued, "Never mind. I'll let you finish your business."

Anon was trying to keep himself together as he went to face off against Zayika. His arms were pulsating with burning hot lightning and his wings carried him over to where she was near the fish. "You should have never killed Amira!"

Hippo let out a powerful wail of emotion which was almost ear-splitting in its volume and tone. The fish's mouth was ajar with sharpened teeth which stood outwards from the rest of her face. The creature knew that Amira died... and she was livid too. Everything became increasingly more intense as Zayika enjoyed creating more devastation. She was finally getting what she wanted. Her eyes were screaming for more bloodshed and strife.

"It's charming that you believe you have a chance to win this ordeal." Zayika turned away from the anglerfish to direct her words at Anon, who was suspended in the air by his massive wings. "But then again, you do have a history of not thinking clearly and choosing to be bold when it can ruin you the most. You inconvenience others, Anon, and honestly? You shouldn't have done anything that you chose to do here on Eunoia. Now you will pay what you owe."

Anon threw his hand in the air, which made Hippo jolt forwards. She pushed heaping amounts of waves and sand in our direction as we tried to run for cover. Anon stayed up high and smiled as the fish made it clear whose side she was on. *Damn it!* I tripped over a pile of mossy rocks and fell face first onto the ground as a rush of waves plummeted over me. I pushed myself upwards as quickly as possible, wanting to check and make sure that Hippo wasn't too close. She got Zayika into her mouth and the rest of us weren't sure what to do but watch on.

"Get me out of this disgusting sea devil!" Zayika's screams echoed. "Get me out!"

Within a few moments, she was able to immerse her body in stars to burn Hippo. The anglerfish roared out again while attempting to crush Zayika. She sent shards of her ability over to its teeth and managed to knock two more of them out right next to where one was already missing.

"Nero! Jameson!" Zayika hollered at us as she got out and fell down into a puddle of water. "How dare you both stand by and not do anything at all?"

"What makes you think that anyone would want to side with you, Zayika?" Anon spoke proudly as the feathers of his wings bounced blue hues off from his arms. "This is between you and me now."

"Not quite." Zekiel spoke.

"This involves us too." Jameson jumped in. "We deserve to fight for what we want."

"What is it that you want?" Zayika's soaking purple hair covered the majority of her white dress as she kicked water out of her boots. "Jameson, I'm talking to you. You have so much potential, are you sure you want to waste it siding with these failures? Have you made up your mind yet?"

Jameson held onto his weapon tightly and stared at Zekiel. "It's time. We know what we have to do, man."

The two became fixated on Anon's wings. *They're going to open up the portal once more… but at Anon's expense this time. There's no way I'm going back in there.* I looked over at Zayika to see if she realized what they were planning to do, but she seemed to not piece it together. *Are they going to send her into it? She will put up a fight, and I'm sure Anon will too. This is why all of them are in this mess… they are unable to think more than one step ahead.*

Zekiel stumbled over to me and pointed to my belt with a quivering hand. It was as if a wall covering his true his demeanor had been broken down, like he couldn't stand disguising himself anymore. I stood my ground as he approached.

"Your knife." Zekiel stated, "Let me have it."

His blonde hair was swaying in the wind and we didn't break eye contact. *Knock it off with shortened sentences and speak your full truth.* Zayika was nearby ranting about Jameson's revealed alliance with the others, but her words sounded muffled as suspense built between my competition and me.

"Do you think I'm gullible?" I asked him. "Why in my right mind would I hand over my weapon to you?"

To my surprise, Zekiel almost grinned. "This will probably be the last time we ever speak to each other, so let's just be honest. You haven't been in your right mind since you got here. No one who is would have done what you did."

"You seem very positive that you can get rid of me. If you want to fight for who will get to see the representative, then fine, let's do it."

Wind began to escape from all of my pores as I cracked my knuckles. The drive in me to survive seemed to have enhanced my ability. I felt air escaping through my entire body. My face, arms, and legs were especially frigid as my mouth grew dry.

Zekiel shuddered and shook his head. "You've got this wrong. I don't want to fight you."

"You're lying to me." I responded with conviction. "Let's get this over with and stop playing verbal games that are unrelated to what's really going on here. Ignite your flames!"

"No you don—"

"Come on, Zekiel!" I tried to convince him to challenge me properly. "Don't worry, I won't force you into the portal this time. I don't want to go back in either, believe it or not."

"That's not it." His voice was weak.

"Zekiel, please hurry! What's taking so long?" Jameson interrupted our conversation to call out after him.

He kept his eyes looking into mine. "This isn't about you and me. What needs to be done is much more important than the words we keep exchanging with each other, Nero. You don't deserve to be let off easy... but I don't have any more energy to give you."

"What does that mean?"

"Give me your knife."

"Why?"

Zekiel swiftly dove past my arm, and with flames coming from his hands, he burnt the side of my chest to grab one of the last blades I had with me. He headed straight for Anon without saying another word. I touched the stinging gash and cursed at him under my breath. *Who does he think he is?*

"Looks like you need some help!" Zayika was peering over her shoulder at me and sent a ray of yellow stars across the shore in my direction.

Why would she look out for me? The scrape was healed in seconds and I felt a surge of power race through my veins. "Thank you!"

"Don't waste words." she replied. "Come show me how thankful you are by helping me take care of the others here."

Of course she has to have something in return. Screw off.

Jameson launched a grenade at Anon, who was suspended in the air. He almost noticed too late, which made him crash land in order to avoid being struck by it. Zekiel sprinted over to him without hesitation with my throwing knife in his right hand.

"Wait! Guys! Let's do this a different way!" Anon looked regretful. "There has to be a different way!"

"You aren't running away." Zekiel said as he stood over him. "Get up."

Jameson went over to both of them and helped Zekiel wrestle Anon away from the ground. Holding onto the stolen weapon, Zekiel latched onto one of his black wings and began cutting into the other. Anon screamed out in pain and tried to get them off of him. Zayika and I didn't interfere at all as they messily hashed out their plan.

"Wait! Don't do this! Please stop!" Anon pleaded while trying to electrocute his former friend.

"We need to open the portal!" Zekiel and Jameson responded in unison without hesitation.

"What are you all doing?" Zayika began glaring. "You aren't getting me in there if that's what you think!"

So much of Anon's blood was spilling onto the ground. The scars on my back began to sting at the memory of Saylor doing the same thing to one of my wings, and how it felt when Zekiel removed the other. *Sorry you're going through this too, Anon. I know exactly what it's like.* I did feel bad for him, but I knew that it wasn't my place to step in between the fight—that was something a person like Omar would do. I knew my place. Zekiel was able to counteract Anon's attack with palms of fire long enough to hack away completely at his wings. Blood gushed from Anon's back as the black hole emerged once more. As they were all about to disappear into it... I almost looked away. *Back up. Don't get sucked in.* Zekiel gave Jameson an apologetic look as he got closer to the whirling entrance.

"Are you serious, Zekiel?" Jameson spoke up. "What are you doing? You don't have to go in there! That was never part of the plan!"

Zekiel stared downwards. "I have to do this."

"Why?" I asked him.

"Look at Amira's body over there." he replied brokenly. "We all are going to meet our demise sooner or later. The loss of those that we care about only results in us losing more of ourselves. There's no point in fighting anymore."

What I say next is crucial. In that moment I had to put aside my past with Zekiel and try to talk him out of reentering the void. "That's not true, alright? Your life... still has meaning."

He gave me his undivided attention. "Tell me what that is."

"Keep fighting. Fight me or Zayika."

"I'd love to see him try." she chimed in.

"I'm being honest." I stepped over to him and didn't look at anyone else. *Why do I care so much right now? Zekiel isn't my friend, but I can't stand to watch this. I want him to take his anger out on me... not give up.* "Fight me. Feel the adrenaline that will course through you when you do. Enjoy what it's like to be alive, even if it hurts. You are alive right now in this challenge. I'd rather you try to defeat me instead of seeing you defeat your own self." *Do not give up, it's the worst thing to do.*

Zekiel inhaled sharply. "There's no point anymore Nero. I simply cannot take what life has to offer me. The cards I got dealt were cursed as soon as I laid my hands on them. I found an escape room. The void is a beautiful place. I will be at peace there."

"That is not peace." I tried to argue. "Peace is living for those who you lost."

"You took one of them from me. Don't you dare try to be supportive now. You are a parasite."

I frowned. "I know that I took Saige's life away, alright? But it doesn't mean that you have to take yours too. Try to fight and defeat me to get back to Earth. Spite me in her name."

"You'll never understand. I can't waste anymore of my time trying to make you see the truth. The portal is about to close. Good luck on your endeavors, Nero, you're going to need it." He looked at all of us before going to step in. "This is where I belong."

Before we knew it... he was gone. What happened was something that I thought I would never see again. Anon was desperately trying to get away from the warped force yanking after him. He ran and gripped onto the closest rocks he could find. Jameson got a hold on him and was able to create enough distance away from it too while Zekiel willingly went inside.

"He was too far gone." Zayika said in a dull tone. "Don't worry, Anon, I won't let you go like that. Maybe it's where Zekiel belongs, but you don't."

"The plan is ruined." I heard Jameson say to himself exasperatedly. "There's nothing I can do about this... where is the representative?"

The portal closed itself after a few more moments and it was time for the final confrontation between Zayika and Anon. She pulled him towards her against his will so that they were directly in front of each other. Jameson and I stood in the shadows and watched with morbid curiosity at what was going to happen next.

"What do you want your last words to be?" she asked him. "I'll let you think for a moment."

Anon responded with hostility, "Zayika. You destroyed everything because you couldn't let go of something."

"You don't think that you're the one who 'destroyed everything'?" She grinned.

"How could I be?"

"Why didn't you let all of us know about the existence of Wish Carriers? If you really cared about the five of us like you claimed… why didn't you inform everyone? I heard you talking to Omar about the truth from the hallway. Then you spoke to Amira, but you didn't include me. Why didn't you tell the rest of us?"

"Zekiel felt no loyalty to anyone besides Saige. The two of them would've only looked out for themselves and their faction. I was close with Omar and Amira."

"Clearly. But why did you not include me? What did you have against me so strongly? I saved your life in the ocean and was also in your faction. I helped us sneak into the Land Dweller's courtyard, I healed the gaping wound in your leg, I—"

"Zayika, I am sorry."

"No one wanted to include me from the start. Even though I was the most level-headed out of everyone, the only one who didn't think purely based on rash emotions and possessed abilities that were completely overlooked."

"You are untrustworthy and rude. You've made yourself out to be a shell of a person. Now that shell has been filled with too much of the worst possible kinds of emotion. Your only goal is to seek out revenge and wreak havoc. I've always sensed a deeper… terrifying side to you. How you are behaving now only proves that my gut-feeling was correct this entire time."

Zayika looked at her fingertips and spun some stars on them. "Fair enough. I've always believed that actions should have consequences, that others should return favors, and I believe I was appointed to deal your sentence out here on this planet."

"You killed Amira for no reason at all! You're as destructive and powerful as an unrelenting tornado! Wake up, Zayika! We are not in a dream!"

"I've been awake for a very long time. Nothing has ever been clearer to me than it is right now."

Zayika's fingers looked like glow sticks as she charged her ability. Anon crouched over in pain while she went and healed the open gashes in his back. "I can't let you bleed out yet, that's why I'm doing this."

Sparks started to fizzle from the lightning in his arms. "You're a twisted person, Zayika."

"It takes one to know one." she responded.

"Whose side are you on?" I asked Jameson while nervously biting the divot in my tongue.

"Neither." He rubbed his forehead and also watched the other two fight. "The plan we had clearly fell through. I shouldn't have tried to side with them at all in the first place. It would've been better to find the representative by myself. I'm just ready to use this wish and get to Earth."

I turned my head towards him slowly.

Wait. He's a Wish Carrier?

Jameson looked petrified momentarily, like he didn't mean to say those words out loud.

I know what I need to do.

Three Months Before

Nero's friends gathered at the rushing waterfall during a warm sunset. The group of four were looking forward to trespassing on the property after hours to swim without getting caught. His twenty-fourth birthday ended up becoming one of the worst days of his life.

"Guys, I'm getting a bad feeling." Taya spoke timidly.

"Oh come on." Nero pulled his shirt off and threw it on the ground. "We aren't going to get caught. Even if we do, who cares?"

"I agree." Hazel replied. "Don't be so scared for no reason. You've been saying all day that you wanted to come with us."

"I know. I just feel like somebody's watching us. I don't know how to describe it." Taya kept looking behind her.

"Sounds like you need to just get in!" Michael shouted as he shoved her abruptly into the freezing water.

"Hey! That's not cool, dude." Nero said sarcastically. "Her cellphone is in her pocket. You wouldn't want it ruined!"

"You both are awful." the last person in the group, Anna, said matter-of-factly as she jumped in after Taya.

The two came out with soaking wet clothes and angered expressions. Nero pulled his smartphone out to take a photo of them, unable to control his snarky laughter. "This is hilarious! You both should see your faces right now! Don't worry, I'll get a picture so you can check it out lat—"

Before he could finish his sentence, Taya grabbed his smartphone and chucked it off into the forest. "Screw you, Nero."

"I didn't even push you in! That was Michael!" he responded defensively.

"I don't care. You could've helped me, but you made Anna do it instead."

Nero said while putting his shirt back on, "Well great. Now the night is ruined and I have to go find my phone." He trudged into the cluster of trees before him. "What an over dramatic bitch." he said under his breath after shooting one more look in Taya's direction.

"You're a miserable person, Nero, and you will always be one!" she called out as he walked away.

Michael called out after him, "We're leaving to head somewhere else. This outing was a bust."

"Fine. Go ahead without me." Nero threw his arms up. "I'll use what little daylight there is left to find my phone since you all don't care enough to help me look."

"You wouldn't help us either." his friend said while leaving him in the dimly lit forest. "Good luck."

The four left Nero alone to fend for himself and retrieve the missing item. He sighed in annoyance as the sun became completely hidden and nightfall arrived. The sounds of rushing water sounded farther away compared to earlier. *He didn't think he traveled a huge distance…* While deciding to give up and head home, a tree branch snapped quite close to him.

"Who's there?" he asked courageously. "You all are such losers if you're trying to prank me."

As he stepped forward there was another snap, but it was louder this time. He shook his head and tried to not get worked up about it. *He briefly questioned why he chose the types of friends he did in the first place.* After what felt like a few minutes, Nero could eventually see the parking lot lights. He checked his pockets and was thankful that he still had his keys on him. With plans to go back in the morning to search for his phone, he took them out and headed for his car.

"You've been chosen." a voice in the dark told him.

Nero was tripped by the stranger and fell downwards in one hasty movement, resulting in his face hitting a jagged rock. "What the hell? Ow, who's there?" He lightly touched a bleeding cut directly below his right eye.

The forest started to light up as a man hunched over him. "It's time for you to leave this place and go where you are meant to."

He flipped onto his back. "Leave me alone! You don't even know me!"

The stranger grabbed Nero's hair and began pounding his head sideways against the rock over and over again. "Don't make this difficult. If I was forced to go there, then you will be too!"

"Screw off!" Nero quickly grabbed his keys and attempted to shove them into the man's eyes, several were jutting out from in between his fingers. "Get away from me or else I'll make you regret your actions!"

Nero's arm was grabbed and electrocuted. He cried out in pain as he hunched down, clinging to his skin as the attacker didn't let go of him but spoke, "It's surprising that you're fighting back—especially compared to the first one. Gebu is not going to last long there. At least you have some tenacity."

"What the hell is in your arms, man, how are you doing this to me?" was the last sentence that Nero spoke right before the man used his free hand to pick up a large rock and knock him out.

"All your questions will be answered soon. Good luck getting back to Earth."

Present

I saw Jameson realize how he had become my primary target. He tried to give a forced expression of cluelessness, like he didn't trust his own words and that he was joking. *I'm not falling for it.* The only joke would be if I believed he didn't mean it. *He has a wish, there's no doubt about it. I have to get it and track down the representative again. It's time I go back home once and for all.*

All I wanted was to see my family again, return to the life I once knew, and have my feet on familiar ground. If Jameson didn't cooperate with me, then he would be in my way of accomplishing what needed to be done. I mentally prepared myself to speak with him. *I hope he doesn't make things difficult. I don't want any more bloody endings, just to be rescued.*

"You know who was supposed to lead us, the starting six, from the beginning?" Zayika asked while spinning around her enemy. "I was. You never led any of us."

"Neither of you did." I said to Zayika and Anon. "It seems that you both were so busy focusing on your own priorities that you didn't look at the bigger picture here."

"That doesn't matter now." she responded.

"So..." Anon spoke up. "Is this really the end?"

"Yes." She took a few steps towards him and finally came to a halt. "So, do you have any last words?"

He thought before responding. "I guess not. I don't know what to say."

"Oh come on. You're always running your mouth faster than you can think. You can muster up something."

Anon bit his lip as he continued, "I'm filled with hopefulness. If I lose this against you, I'll just say that I hope... Amira, Omar, and Saige rest in peace. I hope my family back on Earth will be okay and won't think I abandoned them. I hope Amira knows how much I loved and saw light in her, that Omar knew I was his friend, that Saige felt cared about, and I want Zekiel to truly be in the place he's always dreamed of. And for us? Well, Zayika, I hope that you are happy with what you've done. I can't say I'm perfectly okay with all of my decisions, but seeing as though this is the end of the road, I have to accept the past. I am happy with what I've chosen thus far and who I decided to do it for. I have no regrets."

A single tear started to fall down Zayika's face. "Alright then."

"You aren't just angry, are you? You are upset. I can tell." Anon looked overwhelmed. "You are hurt... aren't you Zayika?"

"You still don't understand who I am? I am crying because I'm happy. Ending you, Amira, and everything else is like having a torturous itch finally scratched. I will finally be able to breathe." She wiped the tears away. "This is over now."

Anon also began crying, though his emotions were clearly of anguish, not joy. "Amira..." his voice was too weak to finish the sentence.

Stars swirled around everywhere from her hands and the ocean and sky were purple. She used her current to wrap up Anon's torso and pulled him closer as he used his arm of lightning to grip onto her. His eyes were entirely drained of energy as he charged up one last bolt. He dug into her neck and tore out her throat as fast as he could. She was stunned. Jameson and I both shielded our eyes from the outpour of light as her ability collided against his. At the same time he tore her neck open, she disemboweled him without hesitation. A stinging ray of her light sliced open Anon's flesh and his internal organs hit the ground in a blood covered pile. She was so busy killing him that she neglected to heal herself. I looked away. I shook at the sight of the two demolishing one another. My teeth chattered as I moved near Amira's body lying still on the ground. Hippo was letting out a low steady hum while sitting next to her. *Her creature is mourning.* Anon's eyes were on Amira right before all signs of life completely left them. Before Zayika was fully gone, it seemed as though she was somehow looking at her own self with a smile planted on her face. Within what felt like an instant, the two were gone.

In that gruesome moment it seemed as though I witnessed one of life's greatest lessons. *This planet's purpose has been revealed. What was it that really mattered to each person who was brought here? How willing were we all to sacrifice our own selves to satisfy never-ending and inhumane selfish cravings that we desired?* All I really ever wanted was to get back to living out the rest of my days on Earth. I would never forget those I killed, but I knew my entire existence would have ended if I didn't fight for it.

I looked at Jameson who was the last one with a wish. He was resting down on his knees, trying to comprehend everything that had just happened.

"Jameson." I walked over to him.

"Nero."

"You have the only wish left." I lightly grabbed onto the final throwing knife in my pocket. "What are you going to do with it?"

His eyes told me his answer before he said it aloud. "Go home."

I replied uncomfortably, "I know this will surprise you, but can you please wish for me to get back to Earth too? Like Anon and Amira should have done for Zayika?"

"You aren't going to hurt me?"

"I don't really want to. I think we can settle this without shedding more blood. What do you think?"

Jameson carefully stood up while grabbing a hold of his grenade launcher. "Are you playing a trick right now?"

The answer to his question was easy. "I'm not. I don't know what others have said about me, but honestly, I waited a while for the game here to begin. I practiced self-defense alongside Gebu, Mae, and then those who came after us. I knew the only way I could survive was to hunt or be hunted. I have now seen the worst qualities this planet could bring out in someone. All Zayika wanted to do was hunt and seek revenge. Anon and Amira… they only cared about protecting each other because of their love. But Jameson, you should believe me, I know I've acted rash in the past, but right now… all I want is to get back to where I should be. Please trust my words."

I was telling the truth and thought he noticed that as he timidly looked at me. "I'm not sure that I can. I really don't know you."

I sighed. "Please… let's go find the last representative and get out of this dreamworld together. I haven't gotten to properly rest in a very long time, and even back on Earth I'm sure I will be plagued by nightmares."

Jameson shuffled back and forth as he thought. "I don't trust you."

That's very unfortunate… because I cannot be stuck here forever. I accepted his choice and did what I felt I needed to without pleading any further. I picked up the air surrounding him, making him turn into a tornado of fear. My eyes closed as I held back the only tear I almost shed on Eunoia. *Damn it, Jameson, I do not want to do this.*

"I will kill you!" he shouted. "I know who you really are, the others told me! I can sense it!"

I resisted the urge to cry as I jumped up to balance myself on the wind and used one arm to get him in a headlock. "I have to do this!"

He tried to wrestle me away from him. "Get off!"

"I'm going to make this quick." I informed him. "I won't make you suffer."

"Don't kill me!" He tried to get a hold of his launcher that was activated beside him, but he was unable to since his hands were occupied with wrestling mine.

"I won't kill you if you decide to save me too." I kept my voice from wavering. "So, what is it going to be?"

I got a tighter hold around his neck and was on the verge of completely cutting off his airway.

"Forget it! I'm not going to let you screw me over, that seems to be what you enjoy doing here. I'm fighting for myself!" Jameson tried to be as brave as he could. "I refuse to be tricked and left for dead with you stealing my wish too!"

He doesn't understand… it doesn't have to be this way. We could both be free.

"It wouldn't play out like that." I told him while remaining suspended in a whirlpool of discomfort.

"I don't trust you. I'm going to look out for myself!"

"One last chance." I warned him.

The wind grew stronger.

"I'm not going to risk everyth —"

With my free hand I jammed my knife into the back of his neck. "I am sorry."

Jameson was in agony and fell down onto his chest. I couldn't see his expression, but I didn't want to. The fire in me that was ignited when I arrived on the planet had been extinguished. My hands were bloody as I wiped them off onto my pants and screamed into the brisk morning air. The storm was starting to subside and colors of the sky were becoming normal again. Intense dark hues of purple were fading away. *I need to find the representative.* I knelt down for a moment and placed my hand over Jameson's body. A small light enveloped my hand as I watched it in awe. *His wish is now transferred to me.*

Every step I took while leaving the ocean felt like a victory march. I was determined to find the bunker again and had to get my bearings. *I can't run out of time or lose this wish.* The field came into view and I couldn't see around it. The stems couldn't get in my way, I wouldn't allow myself to become lost in its maze again. My skin was scratched and tickled as the wheat brushed up against me. *I'm almost there.* It was difficult to not think about all I did and observed. *I have to be close to the jungle by now.* Minutes kept passing. All of the wheat looked the same. *Wait, am I going back the way I came?* I was dizzy and dehydrated. I couldn't keep track of how many hours had passed since eating or drinking. *There will be supplies in the bunker, keep going.* I stopped for a moment and looked in every direction. Only prickly wheat was next to and above me. *Ugh, come on, I didn't make it this far only to die in a stupid field of wheat.* It started raining again as I kept traveling. I could no longer see the clouds or blue lightning that was crackling continuously, but the raindrops were refreshing.

Then suddenly, after a while, I finally made it to the jungle area. I was a bit disoriented from expending so much energy by walking in circles that I ended up in a spot I was unfamiliar with. *Where is the faction building? Did I pass it? I need water.* While holding onto my cramping stomach, I eventually came across a ginormous pond. I was unsure if the water was safe to drink. I crouched down closer and saw how murky it was and that mold was growing within the grass on its edge. *Gross.* The ground below me started shuddering and a creature was making its way out from the pond. An otherworldly crocodile was facing me, it's purple eyes beaming and rows upon rows of spiky teeth shimmering in the light. *I must be hallucinating. This is some sort of fever dream.*

"Do you know where the bunker is?" I asked. *Why the hell am I talking to this thing?*

It gave me a warning growl and started to lift itself up out further from the water on gigantic bumpy legs.

"Screw this. Not today." I turned around and mustered enough stamina to get away from it, and picking my battles wisely, decided to leave it well enough alone.

I used my ability of controlling the wind to help myself move faster in my search for the bunker. Soon I recognized bushes and pathways of dirt. *It can't be far from here.* I finally approached the hidden location near the Land Dweller's faction to find the other last person alive on the planet. My hands were clammy and warm sweat formed all over my face. *Please tell me this is going to work. She has to be here, she has to be able to take me home and willing to grant my wish. I earned this.* The door to the bunker was surprisingly open and I rushed inside. I clamored excitedly while going down each step trying to see if she was there.

"Hello?" my voice cracked. "I'm looking for the Over Ground representative."

I didn't see her as I spun in a few circles, noticing crates and plastic containers stacked high against each wall. There was another room with a shut door that I knocked on.

"What do you want?" she asked me.

"I'm the last person here." It wasn't until I said those words until I realized that my mission was almost complete. "Everyone else has passed."

"Zayika is gone?"

"Yes. She destroyed everyone else including herself. You don't have to be afraid anymore." I helplessly put my hand against the rusted door. "Please speak to me face to face." I hated sounding so desperate, but at that point it's what I had become.

She opened the door with a puzzled look on her face. "Nero. You're still alive."

"After getting out of the void I still managed to find a way off of this planet." I paused. "Wait, you remember me?"

"The Oceanic Guardian's representative, Lorelai, saw a lot of promise in you at the opening ceremony when you made your presence known. You've always stood out as a strong contender. I was happy that you were assigned to my faction."

"Even though I started killing others before the trumpets rang?"

"You were the most determined." She gave me a proud smile, "Look where it has gotten you."

My eyes searched around the disheveled bunker as I tried to process my dream actually coming true. "It was insane out there on the grounds. It was challenging to not let others, you know, screw up my progress or hold me back from this moment."

"I know. It was supposed to be a challenge. There was always supposed to be battle and sacrifice on this planet. You didn't let the rest win."

Victory felt surreal. I managed to surpass everyone around me and mind my own business enough to actually get it done. *It's time to destroy this dreamworld before I'm forced to destroy anybody else who is brought here.*

I stood tall and refocused my attention on her. "I'm ready to finish what I was forced to start. You can take me back to Earth, right?"

"Do you have a wish?"

"Yes. Jameson's."

There was a brief silence as the representative examined me. "It is unconventional to have someone initiate a closing ceremony before a new game starts, but it seems as though you've won this reward, and there's no one else who can grant it besides me. We have to go outside for me to use my teleportation ability. I'm sure you're ready to put this place behind you."

We walked side by side while exiting the bunker. The afternoon started approaching and the sky was clearer, like a cursed haze had been lifted away from it. I let out a deep breath. *Am I really going home?*

She stood at the front door and put her hands behind her back, anxiously tapping her foot against rocks. "Well, this is it, then. I'm sure there's nothing left for you on this planet."

"What about you? What purpose do you have here?" I struck a nerve with my words. "Do you want to go back to Earth too? What is your name?"

"Theia."

"Well, Theia." I tossed my hands into the air while speaking, "Why don't you leave this place behind you as well? We've both completed our duties, haven't we?"

"I guess so." She tucked a braid behind her ear. "When you're ready… speak your wish and I'll place my hand up to make it come true. Remember that you can wish for anything."

"Anything at all?"

She sighed for some reason. "Yes, whatever you'd like. You can even ask for all of the events that took place here on Eunoia to be reversed and for everyone to be brought back to life."

So much power.

"I'm not going to wish for that."

With a surprised look she spoke quickly, "Really? Why wouldn't you?"

"Everything happens for a reason. Undoing past events or rearranging time will do nothing but result in disaster."

"Fair enough."

I looked at the planet one last time and took in its mystical views. "I wish... for Theia and I to go to Earth with no abilities, so that we can live normal lives, and for planet Eunoia to be demolished once and for all when we get to our homes."

There was a burst of light.

A thunderous voice spoke as starlight spun around me, "This is the end. Amira, Zekiel, Anon, Saige, Zayika, and Omar were chosen as the final six to compete in the game you were assigned to. Eunoia. Six letters. Six callings. Five vowels. Five abilities. There was a way for everyone to go home. Opportunities for peace existed in each faction, but only if they allowed themselves to see it. Jameson was the last Wish Carrier appointed here, and Nero you have won his wish through harnessing your thoughts and taking action. Goodwill isn't captivated unless it is manifested, spoken into existence, and put into practice."

Seven Weeks Later

I sat alone on the beach and rocked slowly back and forth with both knees close to my chest. Memories of the past played as a highlight reel in my head. I was unable to forget about the planet and everything that happened to those who were also brought there. I stared at the rising and crashing waves and felt like the anglerfish, Hippo, was somehow living and killing in the undiscovered ocean before me. *No one here on Earth will believe what I have been through.* The two concave holes in my back had scarred over and were always there to remind me of where I came from. They constantly felt warmer than the rest of my skin and as though a part of me was missing. I played the game and won. I never forgot about Eunoia's Carriers and the echoes of their voices as they fought for their wishes.

THE END

NOVEL EXTRA: CHARACTER POEMS

ZAYIKA
Consequences
Revenge and closure
go hand in hand between us.
You can't just have one.

NERO
Scars
I'm reminded of how far I've come,
and the things I had to do
to get back to where I'm from.

ANON
Blue Trance
My existence was threatened by her stars.
My choices came back to haunt me.

My life was made whole with her love.
My better half stood beside me.

Those I loved, lost, and failed to lead,
would remain in the haunting blue trance of my
dreams.

AMIRA
Waterfall Destruction
Every layer presented a new challenge with worry,
every step on mossy rocks created a new story.
It did not work, my wish was wasted when spoken,
your reversal of dreams resulted in lives being stolen.

Finding love for you and myself after a horrifying
abduction,
my wish left no trace despite the waterfall destruction.

JAMESON
Taking Sides
Asked to choose a side,
though I care for all involved.
But who cares for me?

ZEKIEL
Freedom
As I aimlessly exist there are no worries.
Peace and silence surround me.
I am where I belong.
Finally free.